HER SWEETEST OBSESSION

*Jade Royal*

D1509867

© **2019**
Published by *Miss Candice Presents*


All rights reserved.
This is a work of fiction.
Names, characters, businesses, places, events, and
incidents are either the products of the author's
imagination or used in a fictitious manner.
Any resemblance to actual persons, living or dead, or
actual events is purely coincidental.
Unauthorized reproduction, in any manner, is
prohibited.

*Other Works by Jade Royal*

- Love is Worth the Sacrifice (Completed Series)
- Two Halves of a Broken Heart
- How Deep is Your Love (Completed Series)
- Saved by a Beast (Phoenix Pack Paranormal Book 1)
- Craved by a beast (Phoenix Pack Paranormal Book 2)
- Confessions of a beast (Phoenix Pack Paranormal Book 3)
- Seduced (Her Sweetest Obsession) Part 1

# SEDUCED

There was a volcano embedded within her. A volcano that was slowly becoming active as her heart began to race and her skin became hot to the touch. Her nipples were beads of tight frustration, and her pulsing insides were throbbing relentlessly. She needed her fix. That sexual fix that would cross her eyes and cramp her thighs and leave her in a pool of sweat by the time it was all said and done. She wanted to sing to the heavens when she achieved an orgasm so deep it touched her soul.

Slamming the door of the hotel room, she threw her victim up against the closed door. Her kisses were shallow but effective enough to distract him while she worked on getting his belt loose. He was a hunk of muscle she'd been plotting to take down since the moment they met months ago.

Leaving his lips, she left trails of hot kisses against his neck and collarbone. After loosening his belt, she began to unbutton his dress shirt. Baring his bare chest, she groaned low in her throat as she bit his pectoral. Oh, she could just see herself grabbing onto his huge chest muscles as she rode the hell out of him. He was much bigger than her small body, but she didn't mind conquering a mountain at the moment. Lust and arousal had taken over.

"Slow down Giselle," He breathed. She ignored him and tore at his pants. She created space between their bodies so she could unzip her dress. Unlike him, she kept her outfit simple because she wanted to get out of it as quickly as she could. She stood in front of him in her naked glory, hot and aroused.

"Still want me to slow down?" She asked, fondling her own breasts for his pleasure. When he could only stare, she smiled as she closed the space back in between them. Taking his hand, she placed it directly onto her weeping vagina, needing him to touch her. When he slid one finger into her, she moaned running her nails across the skin of his chest. She rode his finger, aiming for a release that was all too ready to be sprung loose. But just before her climax mounted her body, he removed his finger. Getting ready to cuss him out, he silenced her with a kiss.

"Don't worry Giselle. I'm going to make you come. But I want you to come on my dick when I fuck you." Actually, she liked the sound of that more.

"So then give me that dick now, Dean," She ordered.

"Take it," He responded. She got down on her hunches and pulled his pants down, tugging his underwear with it. His erection popped from its confines. She stopped in her tracks, frozen as she stared at his penis.

"Don't be too afraid," He said, rubbing his hands through her long curls. "I'll make sure to take it easy." Giselle figured he was under the impression she was frozen because she was impressed. She tried to gulp down her disappointment as she stared at his fully erect 5 inch dick. *Who the hell did he think would be afraid of this?*

"I'll take care of you," He said in a reassuring

tone. Giselle was only about 5'3 and with her young looks, and pretty smile men always regarded her as a woman that needed to be protected or taken care of. When it came it sex, it was like they were downright afraid to break her. It was the reason she'd only been with two men in her life. Every other man she wanted thought she was too soft. In reality, even though she was polite and soft spoken, Giselle loved a good hard fucking. But now here she was, about to fuck the man she'd been dating for months only to see his dick didn't compare to how big and muscled he was. And he had the nerve to think she was afraid? What the fuck?

Taking a deep breath, she calmed her nerves. The last thing she wanted to do was seem shallow, so she looked up at him and smiled. Flicking her tongue out, she licked the head of his dick. He moaned and let his head fall back. In her mind she reassured herself. *It's not about the size of the boat, just the motion in the ocean.* She just hoped the motion in his ocean would stir up a tsunami in her awaiting seas.

In one motion, she took his cock all the way into her mouth. It barely hit the back of her throat but she let the small dick factor go. She'd wanted sex tonight, and she was gonna get it, no matter what size he was. But then after sucking him for a minute and not having a burning sensation in her eyes from him hitting the back of her throat was boring her. His size wasn't arousing her and it was definitely taking the adventure out of sucking dick. She stopped and stood.

"Think you can handle it?" He asked her. Giselle was trying to be nice, but if he kept playing like his dick was stamped with the Kunta Kinte seal of approval she was gonna hurt his feelings.

"I'd wrap that up if I were you," She said instead, turning from him and walking to the bed. When he disappeared to the bathroom she clasped her hands together.

"Please make him fuck me so good I'll never judge a man by his dick size again." Getting in the bed, she waited for his arrival.

When he returned he was wearing his condom. Still not impressed, but still not going to say anything, Giselle just laid down. When he climbed on top of her, she wrapped her arms around his neck and kissed him tenderly. He put a hand in between them and found her entrance. He slowly pushed his hips forward as he entered her. She groaned for his satisfaction only. When he'd fully entered her, she tried to lift her legs and place them on top of his shoulders so he could attempt to hit her G-spot but he stopped her.

"Let's stay like this for a little bit baby," He said. She had her doubts but she complied and put her legs down. Placing both his hands next to her head, he raised up and withdrew from her body and thrust back into her. Giselle was waiting for the rush to flow through her body. For a spark to be ignited deep within her. For her ocean to begin roaring to life. Nothing happened. What she felt was the sting of his skin as it slapped against hers, and his hard breaths falling onto her face as he struggled to maintain his breathing.

"Damn Giselle!" He groaned. His pumps picked up speed, making her small body bounce back and forth. Her head hit the headboard each time he thrust into her and so far that was the only stimulation she was receiving.

"Maybe if I get on top I-" She was cut off by his

loud shout and groan as he plunged deep into her one last time. His body stilled as his muscles quivered. Giselle stared at him with her mouth wide open.

"Did you just...did you just come?!" She screeched.

"You felt amazing," He smiled, dismounting her. She stared at him in shock as he got off the bed to throw the condom away. When he came back he climbed back into the bed with a satisfied sigh.

"I didn't hurt you did I?" He asked.

"Hurt?!" She just about shouted. He patted her thigh and closed his eyes.

"I'll be gentle for round two babe. Just let me sleep." Giselle could only stare at him as he shut his eyes. Not only was his dick small, but he was a one minute man. This was truly a game the universe was playing on her. Why couldn't she find a man who was willing to give her the pleasures of the earth she desired without thinking she was just some soft spoken girl instead of the quietly seductive woman she was? Finding that man was probably going to be like finding where the rest of Dean's dick was. Impossible.

## Chapter Two

Through the humid haze of Miami, half naked bodies piled into the main floor of the city's most popular strip club. It was an ordinary Saturday night with a line of men anxiously waiting for the club doors to open. Reign Gibson waited for the strippers to line up horizontally in front of him, so he could look them over all at once. He looked down at his clip board and at the strippers to check who had shown up for their shifts and who hadn't. Just as he got to Khloe's name, she stumbled into the main room adjusting her sequined patterned bra.

"Tardiness my dear, will get you into trouble," He said smoothly. She smiled seductively at him.

"Sorry Reign," She said lowly.

"If she wasn't off sucking your dick, she would

have been on time," One of the other girls snickered. Laughter between the girls echoed in the empty room. Everyone knew that he and Khloe were always sexual partners. In fact, while some of the girls here wanted to fuck with him on that level, Khloe was the only one he did choose to have sex with. He didn't want to become one of those club owners that fucked all his employees. Khloe was the first girl he hired when the club became his and she'd stuck by him when other's hadn't.

"Unless you can suck my dick like she does," Reign began. "I suggest you shut your mouth," Reign said. The laughter died down then.

"That's what I thought." he continued to check his attendance. When he finished he put the clip board down and began walking down the line looking at his girls.

"I don't like that, change it," He said to one girl wearing a body suit. She nodded and walked off.

"Take the wig off," he said to another girl. When he approached Khloe she was dressed perfectly. She was actually the epitome of perfection. If Reign had to realistically settle down with a woman, it would be her. She was anything a man would ask for. That's why it was so easy to maintain his relationship with her.

"Go upstairs to my office, Khloe," he told her softly. All the other girls snickered and began laughing again as Khloe blushed and began to walk to his office. They knew exactly what Reign wanted to do to her,

"Oh shut up," Reign smiled at the women. "It's no big deal."

"It is a very, very 'big' deal according to Khloe," one of them said, holding her hands a part for what she thought would be Reign's dick length. Reign looked at her then walked over. He glared at her for a minute then spread her hands further apart.

"How's that for a big deal," he laughed when her mouth fell open. Reign was always serious when he needed to be, and he didn't tolerate much slack in the work place but he knew when to turn that off. He wanted a certain fear in his workers but he also wanted them to be happy working for him. That was the difference between his club and any other one. He protected his girls and had a good relationship with all of them.

"Anyway, we up in five. Three girls a time on the stage then switch it up after 15 minutes, so on and so forth. You can take on any client you want. Please use caution when you take them to the private rooms. Set your terms. If they do not comply alert security." The girls nodded then turned to talk amongst themselves as they got ready for their night.

When Reign entered his office, Khloe was sitting on top of his desk naked with her legs open. She was surely a beauty in her own right, with a honey touched skin complexion and legs that seemed to stretch for days. She smoothed her brown hair from her face and winked at him. Wanting to feel some sort of pleasure always led him to Khloe. Sometimes that's all it was though. Pleasure. She didn't captivate anything besides his dick and he often had to wonder if that was all there was to his life. Pleasure could only last for so long. What Reign was beginning to learn was that when pleasure was done, there was nothing to cover up the emptiness he felt inside.

********

Giselle piled her cherry pie high with vanilla ice cream. She sliced into the pie and began devouring the sweet treat. She needed this pick me up after her awful weekend. She still gave Dean a chance and every single time he entered her body, he was coming in 5 minutes tops. He blamed it on how good she felt, and while she couldn't disagree with him, his excuse wasn't good enough. Her whole weekend was a disappointment and even though she tried to eat right and exercise, she deserved this goddamn pie.

"Can I have another bowl of ice cream?" Giselle asked the waitress as she passed by. The teen nodded at her and smiled.

"Damn girl." Giselle looked up at her best friend sitting across from her.

"What?" Giselle asked. "I'm hungry."

"You had a stack of pancakes this morning too. I've never seen you eat so much in so little time." Giselle rolled her eyes at her childhood friend. She hadn't told her yet about her weekend and was almost embarrassed to. She knew her friend was dying to know the orgasms on top of orgasms that Giselle had. Sadly, that was the exact opposite of what Giselle experienced.

"Sasha I just have a craving."

"Oh my god, you're not pregnant are you?!" She shrieked.

"Hell no!" Giselle laughed. "We just started having sex this past weakened. And he wrapped it up every time too."

"So what the hell happened this weekend? I mean, I've been waiting by my phone for days and you haven't even sent me a text with good details. I never hold out on you!" That was completely true. Sasha Tyrone didn't hide anything from her best friend.

"Alright fine!" Giselle said. "He took me to a spa resort. So we spent the weekend getting pampered and taken care of. He treated me like a straight up queen." Sasha rolled her eyes and gave her a bored stare.

"Bitch I don't wanna hear about that. I mean, it's great he treats you like royalty but you know damn well I'm ready to hear about his dick game. I mean, the man is all muscle and fitness, tall, and chocolate. Please tell me how he treated you like a queen in that bed!"

"His looks are deceiving," Giselle said. "And I mean that literally, in every sense of the meaning." Her mouth fell open.

"Wait a minute. Are you saying-" She was interrupted by Giselle's phone going off. They both looked at the phone. Dean's picture popped up on her screen. None of them moved a muscle as Giselle let it ring out. She did not want to talk to him at all. Not now anyways.

"Oh no," Sasha said, figuring out if Giselle was ignoring the man something detrimental had happened.

"Oh yes," Giselle sighed. "Tall ass man with a small ass dick," She said. "And you know, I hated to be that female to judge him by his dick size. I get judged by my size all the time. So I tried to give it a chance. Not everyone is gifted with big dick."

"So what the hell happened?" she asked. Giselle rubbed her temples.

"Well, let's just say before I could offer to get on

top, he busted a nut." Sasha's mouth flew open. She turned to find the waitress.

"Where's that ice cream!" The waitress hurried over and placed the bowl in front of Giselle. "Honey, you need a pick me up after that!" She said.

"Exactly," Giselle said.

"So what are you gonna do? I mean, if that was me I would completely cut him off. Small dicks aren't so bad, but if he can't even work it properly what the hell you supposed to do?"

"Honestly I don't know. I was being nice to him the whole time but he kept making comments like his dick was huge. But, he is also a nice guy and I hate to dismiss him simply because he can't fuck. I mean, what if I can teach him some things, ya know?"

"You could try. It couldn't hurt. But I don't think you can ever be happy with him if he doesn't please you sexually." Giselle knew that was right, but she had to at least try to get this man to understand what she needed before just completely cutting him off. Like she told Sasha, he was the man of any woman's dreams and he knew how to treat a woman right.

"Let me just work on him. Too bad until I can get him to do me right, I'm gonna be horny as fuck."

"I have a solution for that." Giselle saw the mischievous glint in her friend's eye and just knew anything she had planned was going to be interesting.

Giselle rolled her eyes when Sasha pulled up to the adult store and parked. Sasha smiled brightly at her.

"Come on! This is my favorite spot."

"Its broad daylight," Giselle said. "You shop for fuck toys in broad daylight?"

"Girl please. Stop being so shy."

"I am not shy!" Giselle snapped.

"Giselle, you're cool as hell. I love you to death but when we go out in public you get shy as fuck. When we kicking it alone or with friends you go all out. But the moment we around people you get shy. That's why people keep saying you so cute and soft." Giselle just crossed her arms. That was completely true.

"But trust me. The moment you get a man that rock your world inside and out, you'll be so confident you won't resort to trying to hide your true self. It don't matter if you look cute and bubbly on the outside. You're still a bad bitch on the inside. And like you said, you haven't orgasmed all weekend. So come on and get a vibrating dick." Giselle loved the bluntness of her friend and wouldn't want her to act any other way.

"Alright fine. Let's get me a vibrating dildo." They shopped around for a whole hour, both of them leaving with a bag full of goodies. Dean kept blowing her phone up, but Giselle needed to get home and use at least three of these toys before she returned any of his calls. Her body needed to be sated and relaxed to even confront him because then she'd blow up and tell him just how bad his sex game really was. Maybe she really was just a nice girl because any other woman would have hurt his feelings already.

# Chapter Three

Khloe gagged as she attempted to swallow Reign's dick whole. She sucked hard, slobbering all over him just the way he liked it. Humming around his length, her mouth vibrated against him to amplify his pleasure. When he gripped a handful of her hair she knew she hit the right spot.

"Fuck," he groaned. She used her teeth to rub against him in the way he liked. His body shivered. Khloe deep throated him again just as he erupted deep in her mouth, sending his release down her throat. Khloe kept sucking and massaging his balls so she could swallow every drop of his sweet release. Reign was unlike any man she ever dealt with. She loved how he tasted and it was evident in the glow of her skin that she never let his sperm go to waste.

When he was completely soft in her mouth, she

slowly pulled him out of her mouth, finally releasing the tip with a pop. When she looked up at him from her place in between his legs, he was resting his head back against his office chair with his eyes closed.

"Reign?" She called out softly. He opened his eyes but didn't look at her.

"What's up?" He asked. She stood. Still wearing heels, she was able to tower over him since he was sitting down.

"Was that good?" She asked.

"I came in your mouth didn't I?" He asked. He did, but Khloe felt unsure for some reason still. Maybe it was because he wasn't a man of affection.

"Yeah but...I just wanna make sure I do you good, ya know?" She walked out from behind his desk and went to his private bathroom in his office. She wet a wash cloth and went back out to him to clean him up. He was still sitting just as she left him with his head rested back against his seat. He didn't move a muscle as she wiped him down. When she finished he tucked himself back into his jeans and sat forward leaning on his desk.

"I thought a good dick sucking would make you more relaxed," she said, seeing clearly that he was thinking hard.

"I am relaxed," he said casually.

"You seem to be thinking about a lot," she said. When he rolled his eyes, Khloe stayed quiet for a moment.

"Any trouble with the girls?" He finally asked her.

"Brielle keeps saying slick shit to me," Khloe responded. "But I'll deal with her." Ever since Reign took over the strip club, Khloe had been working for him. She was always attracted to him and went after what she wanted. Everyone knew she was Reign's girl and they respected her as such. Only thing was, Reign didn't sleep around but he also didn't claim her as his woman. They just slept together. Khloe wanted to get to the next level. She was ready to not just be his girlfriend but to be his wife. They'd talked enough about it to know that Reign would settle down with her if she kept at it.

"Brielle," he chuckled, as if he was remembering

something about her that was funny.

"What?" Khloe asked.

"That girl is a trip. She was in here last night."

"In here for what?!" Khloe could feel her anger starting to rise. To say she was territorial was an understatement. She hated when these floozies was all over Reign.

"What you think she was in here for?"

"You really fucked her behind my back?" She asked him. He turned and looked at her.

"Calm down Khloe. I told you I don't fuck none of these women." Khloe just crossed her arms. Reign could see she was clearly upset. He stood from his desk and went over to her. He uncrossed her arms and kissed her on the mouth. He truly had a soft spot for the woman even though he wasn't necessarily in love with her. He took her by the wrist and pulled her towards his desk, turning her around so her back was facing him, then he placed her hands down flat against his desk. He lifted her short skirt and found she wasn't wearing underwear. He swiped her hair behind her ear.

"What I tell you about walking around with no

panties on?" he whispered in her ear. Even though she was upset with him, of course she felt her arousal begin to peak at feeling his hard body behind her.

"I came straight here when I took them off," she said.

"It doesn't matter." He slapped her firm bottom. She yelped in pleasure at the sting of the hit. He wrapped a hand around the front of her neck and bit her earlobe.

"I don't want you worrying about these other females, hear me?"

"Why shouldn't I worry?" She asked. When she heard his zipper get pulled down, the bottom of her belly quaked with anticipation. Reign was everything a woman could ask for. Especially when it came to sex. He was the best she ever had. That's why she hated the idea of any woman being around him. She didn't want anyone to know just how good he could fuck. She didn't even want any woman simply touching him.

She shivered when she felt his tip brush against her opening. When he slid into her, she gasped and closed her eyes. Arching her back to prepare for more of his large entry, she was disappointed when he stopped his movements.

"Don't tease me Reign," she ordered.

"First tell me what I told you," he said. He pulled out and entered her again but he didn't go past his tip. She tried to grip his tip but he wasn't deep enough.

"You said, you said that if you ever had sex with another woman, you'd tell me." He rewarded her with a couple of inches.

"And?" He coaxed.

"You wouldn't disrespect me by fucking another woman and then fucking me right after." He gripped her neck tighter and entered her fully in one thrust. She grunted loudly as the force of the thrust made her fall against the desk. Reign let go of her neck. He slapped her ass again.

"Arch that back like I like it," he ordered. She did as she was told. He held her cheeks and sunk the last of his length inside her. Literally in the bottom of her stomach, Khloe grabbed onto the desk to hold on, knowing he was about to tear her stomach up.

"When was the last time I made your pussy come?" he asked her. He pulled out slowly and slid all the way back in at the same speed. Her pussy muscles were already quivering.

"Not since last week," She breathed. He pulled out slowly again all the way to the tip, then slid back in to the bottom of her stomach.

"So should I just fuck the shit out of you, or take it easy to make it last longer, huh?" Khloe shook her head wildly.

"No, what?" He asked.

"Not slow," she said. "I don't want it slow."

"Oh I see what you want."

"It's all yours Reign. Fuck it and own it." Never in their relationship had Reign ever claimed her body as his, and she wanted him to. She wanted him to realize the seriousness of their relationship. She was truly his to own.

"Mine to own, huh?" He asked. Before she could reply, he slid out of her again. But his inward thrust was anything but slow. He banged into her insides repeatedly. Bright lights went off behind her closed eyelids as he touched that part of her that was the source of her pleasure. When he slapped her ass again, Khloe understood that he wanted her to arch her back deeper. As she did, he held her at the waist and plunged deeper and deeper. He thrust upwards to where he knew her favorite spot was.

"I'm coming!" She shouted, her legs quivering. He just grunted in response and kept thrusting. When her orgasm rolled over her body, her legs gave out. She would have collapsed if he wasn't holding onto her hips. Without giving her a chance to recover, he kept thrusting inside her. Her ass was bouncing off his abdomen each time he thrust into her. Moisture was dripping between her legs and more was beginning to squirt out. Her eyes rolled to the back of her head when he reached in front of her and pinched her clit. Her orgasm pushed him out as she squirted her release. Since he had let her go and backed away as she came, this time she fell to the floor as her legs continued to shake.

Reign admired his handiwork as Khloe had an orgasmic seizure on the floor in front of him. His dick was literally dripping with her come. He loved pleasing a woman. The sex itself was enjoyable, but seeing a woman in the midst of orgasms and pleasure made the sex all the better.

"Are you okay Khloe?" he asked. She nodded as she fisted the carpet, trying to get herself to stop shaking. He bent over and picked her up carefully before bending her over the desk again.

"I'm not done with you," he said as he kicked her legs open. She reached back, placing her hand against his abdomen as he entered her. That was her sign for him to take it easy.

"I got you," he assured her. Being confident he wasn't going to push her too far, she moved her hand from his stomach.

"Fuck...." She drawled out as he entered her slowly. "It hurts so good," she moaned. Her moans turned into little cries as he pumped her at a slow and steady pace. The head of his dick rubbed against the rough spot inside her making Reign feel his own orgasm load up at the base of his dick.

"Just a little bit more," he groaned as he sped up.

He held her down by placing one hand in between her shoulders. She was starting to squirm and he just wanted her to take his last few strokes and not move. His other hand dropped to his side ready for when he was going to pull out.

"Come for me one more time," he said, thrusting harder. She came on command coating him again and shivering in pleasure. When Khloe heard his grunts as he fucked her harder, she knew he was about to come.

"Come inside me," she said aloud. She sensed a slight hesitation in his stroke but he didn't stop.

"No," he answered solidly. She went to pop up and ask why, but he forced her down and kept stroking her. When he grunted loudly, she felt the loss of his penis inside her, and the hot stream of his release painting the top of her bottom. She stayed quiet as he emptied his release onto her. When he was done, he let go of her back and walked away. Not moving yet, she waited until he returned with another wash cloth to wipe her up. That's when she turned and looked at him.

Reign could see the disappointment in her eyes,

even though she was trying to hide it. They'd been having sex for years and knew each other even longer than that. He'd stopped using condoms after a year or so, but he'd never came inside her. Not even by accident either.

"Why don't you ever come inside me?" She asked him finally. He wiped himself off and tucked himself back in his jeans and zipped up.

"Because I don't want to get you pregnant Khloe."

"I'm on the pill," she said. "And so what if I got pregnant?"

"We're both not ready for that kind of shit," he said. "When we both want to settle down, then we can talk about us having a kid Khloe."

"You're the only one that doesn't want to settle down," she mumbled.

"Excuse me?" he asked, even though he heard her. "Don't turn this shit on me. You forget you're still a stripper? Yet you can stand here and tell me you wanna carry my child?" Khloe stayed quiet.

"You know I'll never disrespect you by what

you choose to do with your life K, but I've asked you countless times to stop stripping. I told you I would take care of you. So if you really want to settle down, you would have done what I asked. I won't treat you any different for being a stripper but I'd be damned if I let you do that shit while pregnant." Even though he was being hard on her, Reign meant what he said. Khloe loved exotic dancing and she was good at it, so he let her do what she want. But dancing with a fetus, his fetus at that was a no go.

"So what, I should just stop dancing for you to want to settle down with me? I'm not good enough because I'm a stripper?" Reign rolled his eyes.

"I've never said that to you Khloe. What I said is that I don't want you dancing on a pole for money with my baby inside you. So, when you're ready to retire we can fuck and I come inside you as many times as you fucking want me to."

"Do you mean that?" She asked. Reign just nodded. He should have second thoughts about saying these things to her or wanting to do things to her but he didn't. He was just accepting reality. Khloe was the only woman he'd actually spent time with and had sex with that lasted over a year. Any other female he met was only going after him for either his money or just sex. Khloe wanted good for him. If he ever wanted kids she was his shot at that. Being the last Gibson left on this earth, he was gonna make damn sure his bloodline lived on. He wasn't in love with her, but he didn't need to be. He was comfortable enough being with her just as they were.

"Okay fine," she huffed. "You're right. We're both not ready yet. I like my body like it is right now anyway. But I am still on the pill. When we have quickies and you pull out it's messy and I hate cleaning up. But if you just came in me, it would be easy." Reign sat back down behind his desk. He gazed at her for a minute.

"I'm still gonna have to decline that offer," he said.

"Why is that?"

"Because I believe when a man comes inside a woman it is his intent to have his seed grow within her. Since I don't intend to do that then I will not come inside you."

"Am I your girlfriend?" She asked. Reign rolled his eyes.

"Imma grown ass man Khloe. That boyfriend, girlfriend shit is for young people."

"So I'm your fuck toy?" Reign gazed at her again, trying not to lose his temper. He didn't have a short fuse, but this woman tested him a lot.

"Didn't I just tell you, like 2 minutes ago that I was willing to make you the mother of my child? Think that's fuck toy privileges?"

"But you don't tell people I'm your woman."

"Why do I have to?" He questioned.

"So they'd stop trying to be with you too."

"You think it matters if I tell people we're together?" He asked. "Because every female in here knows we are but that sure doesn't matter to them." Khloe crossed her arms.

"Yes it would matter."

"So why would Brielle be in here asking to suck my dick when she knows about me and you?" Reign asked. When Khloe didn't answer he nodded his head.

"Point proven." He scoffed as he looked at his watch.

"Make sure the girls are ready for tonight please. You still need to get yourself ready as well."

"See ya later then." She bent over his desk and kissed him on the lips. The kiss was short and quick. Come to think of it, they'd never actually had a deep kiss. Khloe just accepted it as the way he was. Reign was a very simple man that never liked to complicate matters. He wasn't too affectionate but he knew how to show he cared.

"Can you actually bring me back a drink from the bar?" He asked. Khloe scoffed.

"Get yaself a personal assistant for all that shit," she said. Reign rolled his eyes.

"Send Brielle to do it then." She nodded and left his office. The woman wanted to bear his seed but she couldn't even get him a drink. She surely had some things to learn.

Khloe marched straight to the ladies dressing room. The moment she entered, all chatter died down.

The girls stared at her, waiting for her to say something. Being close to Reign, she was the one that always delivered messages.

"Where the hell is Brielle?" Khloe asked.

"In the showers," someone said. When Khloe headed straight for the showers, someone muttered a curse and all the women followed her. Entering the shower area Khloe ripped open the curtain to the only stall that was on.

"What the fuck?!" Brielle shouted. Khloe turned the water off and grabbed Brielle by the hair, pulling her out. She slapped her across the face and dragged her back to the dressing rooms where she tossed her on the carpeted floor.

"Reign told me you were in his face," Khloe spat. "So you tryna suck his dick huh?"

"Bitch please! That's why you mad?" Brielle said, getting up from the ground. "Newsflash, all of us asked Reign to suck his dick at one point! Shit, what woman wouldn't want to suck that man's dick?"

"But you know I'm his woman, how you just gonna straight up disrespect me and mine?"

"You act like you walk around here respecting every damn body. You're a bitch just like the rest of us."

"This is just a warning Brielle. Stay away from Reign. If I find out you keep bothering him to suck his dick I will fuck you up."

"Whatever Khloe. Just know that out of all 20 of us, at least five has already sucked his dick, and hell even one of us got the chance to ride it." Brielle winked and turned to walk away.

"Oh and before I forget," Brielle said, turning back around. She slapped Khloe hard in the face, returning the favor. Khloe just held her cheek, thinking about what Brielle said. She had no idea that one of these girls actually had sex with Reign. He said he would tell her if he ever did that and he hadn't.

The speaker system cut on in the dressing room, and Reign's voice came over the intercom.

"Brielle, I'm waiting for you," he said. The static cut off.

"For what?" Brielle asked Khloe.

"He wants a drink from the bar," she answered.

Brielle giggled and ran off to put clothes on. When she was leaving the dressing room, she only had on a short loose silk dress that showed clear she wasn't wearing any sort of under garments.

"He likes patron, doesn't he?" She called out, leaving the dressing room. Khloe looked around at all the girls staring at her.

"Which one of ya'll fucked him?" She asked. No one said anything but she saw one of the girls turned slightly away from her and smile. Khloe just nodded, now she knew who the sneaky bitch was.

"Okay I see how it is. Oh well." She left it at that, but she still had a plan. As she left the dressing room she saw Brielle with two shots of patron in her hands going up to Reign's office. Deciding she wasn't about to let no average bitch try to clown her, Khloe went up to her.

"Reign called back on the intercom," Khloe said. "He asked you to bring him a shrimp and grits from the kitchen."

"Let me bring these to him first then get it."

"Let me bring it and you get the food. I'll tell

him you're coming." She was hesitant at first, but she handed Khloe the drinks and scampered off to the kitchen. Khloe turned and went back to his office.

"Thought you said I needed a personal assistant," Reign said when he saw Khloe.

"You do. But Brielle went to do something I don't know what. She said bring these to you."

"Why is your face red?" He asked her.

"That bitch slapped me," Khloe complained. "I asked her not to come back asking to suck your dick and she got mad. Then she started ranting about how she could have you if she wanted to. Is that even true?"

"She's not my type K, don't worry about it." Reign's demeanor almost never changed no matter what he was talking about. Nothing seemed to get under his skin enough for him to raise his voice.

"Which was what I told her anyway. Then you came on the intercom. When I told her you wanted a drink she just got downright mad. I don't know, that maybe she didn't wanna be like your maid or something. She stormed out of the dressing room muttering something like 'I'll get him something, alright.'" Khloe shrugged.

"I followed her out and found the drinks on the bar, but I don't know where she went. I knew you were waiting so I just brought them up to you." Reign just shrugged.

"Getting me a drink isn't that big a deal," he said. Khloe pushed his chair back and sat on his lap. He continued to write up invoices while she leaned against his chest and massaged his neck.

Within ten minutes, there was a knock on the door. When he granted entrance, Brielle entered carrying a platter of food from the kitchen.

"Heard you was hungry," she said, even though she couldn't stop staring at Khloe sitting on his lap. Khloe smirked.

"Thanks Brielle," he said. Brielle looked at the both of them. She knew Khloe was trying to push it in her face about her and Reign. But Brielle was close to being able to get her chance with the man.

"Anything else you need Reign?" she asked.

"Actually yes there is. There's a no violence clause in the contract you signed when I hired you," he said.

"Okay," she said, not understanding.

"So you owe me the 150 dollar fine for slapping Khloe."

"What?! But that bitch-"

"150 dollars or I fire you," Reign interrupted. She crossed her arms and rolled her eyes.

"Fine. My money is in the dressing room," she mumbled.

"No worries, pay it before the night is over." She just shrugged.

"Enjoying your drink?" Brielle asked him.

"Actually I am. Thanks for the food as well I was in fact hungry," Reign replied.

"What'd you get?" Khloe asked. She reached forward and pulled off the cover to the food, revealing the steaming bowl of shrimp and grits. Just like she anticipated, Reign shouted and jumped up. Khloe fell off his lap as he darted out from behind the desk and went across the room.

"Are you out of your fucking mind?!" he shouted. Khloe watched as her plan unfolded.

"What-what you mean?" Brielle asked, scared. This was the first she'd ever heard Reign raise his voice to her.

"Get the fuck out!" He snapped. "And I mean, get all your shit and get the hell out of my club!"

"But-what-"

"Khloe call for security," he ordered since the security button was on his desk and he wasn't going anywhere near his desk where the steaming shrimp sat. Khloe called for security with a smirk on her face. When they burst through the room Reign pointed at Brielle.

"Get all her shit, and get her the fuck out my club," Reign ordered.

"How could you do this?!" Khloe shouted at her. Brielle looked around truly confused. "Reign has been nothing but good to all of us. What you thought you was gonna do? Try and kill him?" Khloe saw the wheels turning in Brielle's eyes.

"Everyone knows Reign is deathly allergic to shellfish." Khloe felt utter satisfaction when Brielle finally connected the dots.

"You bitch!" Brielle screeched. "You set me up!"

"Get her the fuck out!" Reign shouted. The security guards grabbed her by the arms and escorted her out.

"Khloe go throw that shit away," he ordered. She picked up the plate of food and ran it out of the office to throw it away. When she returned, Reign was wiping his desk off with disinfection wipes. But already she saw the small spots of hives breaking out on his skin.

"Fuck!" He cursed, looking at his arms. "I'm going home. I'll be back before the club closes. I need to get my medication,"

"You want me to come with you?" she asked, putting on her worried voice.

"No, no. Stay here and watch over the girls." She nodded and watched as he grabbed his car keys and all but ran out of the office. Khloe smiled. She hated putting him in danger like that, but she had to get rid of that bitch. One down, one more to go.

News of Reign not being in the club was going all around. With Khloe being in charge, no one asked her questions or bothered her as she ran errands. When the club was in full swing and all the guards were busy, Khloe went back to Reign's office. There wasn't any camera's in the hall leading to Reign's office or camera's in his office it was easy to take three envelopes of money stowed away in his closet where he kept some of the clubs money and supplies. Since everyone respected Reign no one ever stole from him until now. Khloe took the envelopes and hurried back to the girl's dressing room. She found the bag of the woman who fucked Reign behind her back. She stuffed the envelopes in her bag and left before she got caught.

Khloe kept up with her errands and working with the girls until Reign returned. She could still see the red marks on his arms but he looked fine otherwise. He checked in with all his workers before going to his office to finish his inventory and count his bank. She didn't say anything or see him for the rest of the night. At 4 in the morning, the doors closed to the club. All the girls went to the dressing room to shower and change to get ready to go home. Khloe was nervous about her plan and if it would work. If it didn't, then that meant that woman had free money Khloe had basically stolen for her.

As all the girls walked out, Khloe smiled when she saw Reign standing at the entrance with the security guards next to him. The door was still locked as he leaned against it, not allowing anyone to leave. He looked directly at her and motioned for her to come to him with index finger.

"Are you okay?" She whispered.

"Are you stealing from me?" he asked, ignoring her question.

"Of course not!" She said. "I would never."

"My money is missing Khloe and I left you in charge. I'm not gonna fire you Khloe, so I need you to be honest. Did you take my money?"

"I promise I didn't," she said. He looked at her for a long time then sighed.

"Is everything alright?" One of the girls asked.

"Straight line," Reign told them. They did as he asked. "Is there anyone here who feels like I have done something wrong to them?" He asked.

"Not at all!"

"Do you ladies know why I fired Brielle?" Reign asked.

"Actually, we were all wondering why," Gina spoke up. "You never fire girls."

"She triggered my allergic reaction to shellfish. Something like that could have killed me. And well, I can't work with people I can't trust." Everyone stayed quiet. "Now, the only night where I'm not here, I have money missing. So someone is gonna confess or we'll be here all day." Of course no one said a word. Everyone looked around at each other waiting for a confession but it never came.

"Turn out your bags," Reign ordered. "I don't have time for this shit." No one objected. They all thought they were innocent. When the three envelopes fell from Kate's bag she gasped. Reign looked directly at her and went to stand in front of her.

"I swear I have-" Reign took the envelopes from her.

"Get out and do not come back," he told her.

"But Reign, I-" He turned his back on her and walked away. Khloe followed him immediately. In his office he was sitting at his desk massaging his temple. She went behind his desk and rubbed his shoulders. She smiled when he relaxed against her touch. Khloe would eliminate any female who tried to come between her and Reign. There was nothing she wouldn't do or anyone she wouldn't double cross for the sake of her and Reign's relationship. Both those bitches tried her, and now both of them were gone. Khloe laughed in her head as she kissed Reign's temple and continued to massage his aching shoulders.

Giselle put the finishing touches on the makeup for the last model she was working with. She was a certified cosmetologist that did freelance work for model companies or agencies. She liked the freedom her job gave her and she loved doing hair and makeup. She found that she did better work when she was her own boss. The last time she had a boss, she quit after knocking him in the nuts. To say he was a complete dick was an understatement.

When she finished up her model she packed her things away in her makeup bags and briefcase. She took off her makeup brush apron and packed that away then untied her hair from the ponytail she always put it in and she was ready to go. She went to see the supervisor for the agency to collect her check.

"Fine job you did. Here you are," he said giving Giselle the envelope.

"Thanks a lot." When Giselle looked into the envelop she was surprised to see she'd only made 500 dollars.

"Um, I thought we agreed to 2500 dollars," she said.

"Well at first we did, but I had to make some cuts."

"How come you didn't talk this over with me? I've been working for you all weekend. Three events in a day, 25 models, all with different makeup and you're giving me this? I don't think so."

"Look, ain't nothing I can do okay? So again I thank you for your services. You can leave or I can have security remove you." Giselle just stared at him.

"Dickhead," she scoffed. She rolled her bags out of the office and exited the building. Dean was outside waiting for her like he said he would be, leaning against his car.

"Hey babe," he greeted. He kissed her on the cheek. "You alright?" He asked, seeing the sour look on her face.

"That dick agreed to pay me a 2500 dollars by the end of the week and he cut my whole check more than half without even consulting me. And here, I just did all this fucking work to my best ability and got paid shit for it."

"Wait a minute, you asked him for the rest and he said no?"

"He told me get out or get kicked out. And I mean, I have my dignity so I just left. But still, it ain't right what he did." Giselle pouted and crossed her arms. No doubt he rushed her out like that because he didn't see her as a threat.

"Come on, get in the car." He ushered into the car, and packed her bags in the trunk. Instead of getting in the car with her, he just shut the door and walked back up to the building. Giselle was curious as to what he was about to do but she was still mad so she sat in the car with her arms crossed. She was too dazed out thinking about how she was going to get that idiot to pay the rest of her damn feel. After ten minutes, Dean had returned to the car and slammed the door once he got inside. She jumped from her thoughts and looked at him.

"Here," he said handing her another envelope. When she looked inside it was another check written out for the rest of her money.

"How did you-" Giselle was speechless.

"Turns out he's not so tough." Giselle couldn't help but smile

"Thanks Dean," she smiled.

"Anything for my girl." Her smile disappeared after that. His girl? Not a chance.

"Dean I told you we're not at that level yet," she sighed.

"I know what you said Giselle, but that don't matter. I'm still gonna be there for you."

"Please. You just like fucking me," she scoffed.

"Well there's that too. And speaking of fucking..." Here we go again, Giselle thought. Even though she and Dean were spending time together, she didn't want to commit herself to someone that she was having doubts about. She made that very clear to him so he could understand where she was at. That plus she didn't want him spending money on her because he assumed that would make her his woman permanently. Right now, they were just having fun with each other. Giselle wanted to keep it that way. Especially because she still needed to teach him how to please her.

*****

Giselle pushed Dean off her as his body continued to twitch even after he'd orgasmed. She rolled her eyes at his snoring and shook her head as she walked to the bathroom. Three rounds in one night and each time he seemingly got worse. She was surely about lose her damn patience but she was trying hard not to. Opening her bathroom cabinet she pulled out the dildo she'd bought from the toy store. Hopping up into the counter she spread and legs and slowly got to work. She kept her voice down as she vibrating dildo did Dean's job. Her body shook and convulsed as she came around the toy. Imagine, she had a hunk of a man in her bed, and here she was in the bathroom getting laid by a toy.

She put the toy away and went back into the

room. For some reason, seeing him passed out sleeping like he done a bomb ass job really got her upset. She jumped onto the bed and elbowed him hard.

"Wake your ass up!" She snapped.

"What the fuck girl," he said, rubbing his eyes.

"Get the fuck up."

"What for? You ready for round two?" When she didn't crack a smile, Dean knew she was serious. "What's the matter?" He asked her.

"You need to get up and fuck me 'til I come Dean, and I'm dead serious. You laying here snoring like you just conquered Mount Everest."

"Didn't you just come?" He asked.

"Did you feel me come Dean? Did you even hear me moaning?" She scoffed and pushed him down on the bed, straddling him. She grabbed a condom from the night stand and ripped it open.

"I don't know what you afraid of but you can actually fuck me. You don't gotta give me those timid ass strokes you be doing. I ain't gonna break." He watched with wide eyes as she strapped him with the condom and positioned him at her entrance. She slid down in one motion and he immediately grabbed her hips.

"Be careful," he urged.

"Get your hands off me Dean. Now." He slowly took his hands off. She rested her palms against his chest and began riding him. She clenched him tight and didn't stop or slow down no matter how much he protested. Feeling a tingling at the base of her spin she was so ready to come.

"Damn baby that's so good," he groaned. His closed his eyes and tilted his head back. She could feel his body twitching already.

"Don't you dare come before me," she ordered, rocking back on him harder and faster to achieve her orgasm before he did. But all her efforts were in vain. He grabbed onto her hips and shouted out as he came again. He jerked uncontrollably, shouting to the heavens as if his soul was just snatched. Giselle crossed her arms and sat on top of him lifelessly and allowed him to ride out his orgasm as he jerked his hips up. When he finally fell flat against the bed he was closing his eyes again and humming sweetly.

"Are you satisfied now?" He asked. "Damn that was some good fucking." Giselle just stared at him. It was like he was completely oblivious to what she wanted and he didn't seem to care. He was all for himself.

"You're a selfish bastard," she grunted, getting from on top of him angrily. "Get your shit and get out," she ordered.

"Wait, what for?" He asked.

"Just get out," she sighed. "Hope you had a good fucking nut." She could hear in her own voice how bitter she sounded. How else was she supposed to deal with it. Dean just point blank refused to care about learning anything she was trying to teach him for the sake of both their pleasures.

"I'll talk to you some other time," She said as she retrieved her short satin robe to cover her naked body. After looking at her for a long time, Dean finally got the picture that she wasn't playing around. He slowly got out of the bed and began getting dressed. Giselle watched him from afar with her arms crossed. When he was dressed he walked over to her and attempted to kiss her. She immediately moved her face from his.

"See ya around," she told him.

"You not gonna tell me what's the problem?" he asked.

"Nah I'm good. You had a good nut that's all you seem to care about. No reason to talk about anything else. So yeah, I wanna take a bath and get some rest so..." He sighed in disappointment before he left her small one bedroom place.

When she heard her front door open and close, she let out a frustrated sigh and went to her bed, flopping down like a dead fish. Even though she told Dean she wanted to take a bath and get rest that was the last thing she wanted to do. Looking at the time, it was nearing 11. For a Friday night that was significantly early. She needed to do something where she didn't feel like a complete reject because of her sex life.

"I need drinks," she told Sasha, the moment her best friend picked up the phone. "A couple of drinks as a matter of fact."

"Wow, that bad huh?" Sasha asked.

"I was so close. So close. I had to get a ride out of my damn vibrating toy but I wanted to see if I could get Dean to actually be the one to satisfy me. But the selfish bastard didn't even try to hold out for me. How the hell could one man be so damn oblivious?"

"I told you to forget about that man but you insisted you could make something work. And now look, he got you all worked up." Sasha scolded her. Giselle ignored her.

"Get dressed, I'm gonna pick you in in an hour," she said instead.

"Okay fine with me. Wear something sexy. Maybe you can pick up a man that can actually fuck you right," Sasha teased her.

"This is all your fault! If you hadn't told me to take his number in the first place then I wouldn't be sitting here sexually frustrated."

"Girl, use that damn dildo before you pick me up. I am not dealing your attitude," Sasha said.

"I used that dildo and guess what? That shit just got me extra angry. Especially when I came out and saw him knocked out, snoring all fucking loud too. So that's the last time I am taking any advice for your ass." Sasha laughed loudly. Giselle chuckled herself.

"Anyway, be ready."

"See ya," Sasha sang before hanging up. Giselle hung up the phone and went to her closet. She wasn't necessarily going to dress up that much before, but now that Sasha mentioned it she was thinking about it. She wasn't aiming to fuck anyone else tonight but maybe just looking sexy and having men drool over her might make her feel better about herself.

She decided to wear her favorite black shorts and a simple black halter top that showed off her stomach, and the vines and roses tattoo going up the side of her back. It was terribly humid outside, so she just left her hair long and curly. Any hairstyle she would have done would just end up as a hot fuzzy mess anyways. Dressed with a small touch of makeup, Giselle stepped into her black pumps and she was ready to go out into the night.

It took her 15 minutes to drive out to Sasha's condo. With just one beep, Sasha came out of the house carrying two shot glasses. The woman didn't have any shame whatsoever. Giselle glared at her when Sasha hopped in the car.

"Here," Sasha said giving her the shot glass. "Patron!"

"You are crazy bringing me that while I'm bout to drive!"

"Well, looks like you better down it quick before you get caught sippin," Sasha winked. Giselle laughed before quickly downing the shot. One shot wasn't going to hurt her. It burned deliciously in her chest, powering her up for the night. Sasha downed her drink and clapped.

"Now let's go shake some ass and take some numbers!" Sasha cheered. Giselle shouted in excitement as well as she pulled off and drove towards the famous Miami strip that would give them entertainment all damn night.

**\*\*\*\***

It was nearing 1 in the morning when both girls stumbled out of a bar and lounge. They were sweaty and drunk as they laughed and tripped over each other.

"Did you see that tall chocolate man staring at you?" Sasha asked, fixing her bustier top so her boobs weren't hanging out.

"I saw him alright. But he was too much of a fly guy to talk to me I guess," Giselle shrugged.

"Not like he could get the chance. Seemed that every damn man in there was all over you." Though she was receiving attention, none of the men had hit it home for her. There was just no spark. Then again, like she said before, it wasn't like she was aiming to fuck anyone new but she was still yearning for something better than what she had in Dean. She didn't quite know exactly what she wanted from a man, but she believed that she would get her answers when the time was right. What she did know right now however was that she found herself not being attracted to any of those men who hit on her. She was attracted to Dean, but only in a small way that allowed herself to sleep with the man. But that small ounce of attraction was slowly diminishing with the way the sex was diminishing. Not like it was built up in the first place.

"Oh wait, let's check this place out!" Sasha said, pulling on her arm. They stopped and looked up at a large strip club building.

"Really? A strip club?" Giselle was doubtful she wanted to be inside that place.

"Yes! Do you know how long I've wanted to come and dance for this place?" Sasha was a freelance professional dancer just as much as Giselle was a freelance cosmetologist. Wherever she could get dancing gigs, Sasha was on it.

"So you wanna get on the pole now?" Giselle joked.

"I don't see why the hell not. Everybody selling their souls to the pole now. So can I," Sasha grinned.

"Well why haven't you come and danced here before?"

"This is one of the hardest places to get into. I've heard stories and I chicken out. Let's just go and check it out though. I heard they have bomb ass chicken wings on the menu." Giselle shrugged. They slung their arms over each other's shoulders and walked sloppily towards the entrance.

"Are you ladies here for the openings?" The security guard asked them as they tried to pay to enter.

"Um, no. Just here to enjoy the shows. But there are openings to be a dancer?" Sasha asked. The guard nodded.

"You should check it out. Talk to any one of the dancers if you're interested." Giselle looked at her friend as they entered. She was beaming.

"You should definitely dance for them then. What are the chances there's an opening? When we just so happen to finally come to this place?" Giselle told her.

"True, but I'm nervous," Sasha said twiddling her thumbs.

"How bout we just go and have a good time then let's just see what happens?"

"I like the sound of that."

The large club was crowded with half naked bodies with flashes of lights that painted the room in a colorful glow. The patrons of the club were both equally men and women. The second floor balcony contained the private dancing areas sectioned off by red velvet ropes, and a number of private rooms with red doors that were all closed. Giselle could only guess what the hell happened in those rooms.

"Look," Giselle said into Sasha's ear so she could hear over the music. "If you work here, I don't ever want you in dem rooms with some random ass horny man." Sasha laughed and pinched Giselle on the arm.

"I hear ya sista." They held onto each other as they went to the bar. After ordering drinks, they found a cocktail table where they ordered wings. As they waited for the food, they turned their attention to the stage where three dancers were performing. Giselle could tell Sasha was really feeling the atmosphere. The woman couldn't sit still. Every song that came on she was moving her shoulders or bouncing around dancing. When their food came, she didn't even stop dancing as she ate.

"You ladies look like you're ready to have a good time." A man came to their table, putting himself in between them. Giselle looked at him and just rolled her eyes. It took something that simple to get her annoyed.

"Go away," she stated. Sasha sipped her drink.

"I agree. Go away," Sasha added. The man looked back and forth between them shocked he was turned down.

"I got money ladies, no worries." He pulled out a wad of money and flashed it at them. Rearing back, Giselle was two seconds away from punching him straight in the face before a security guard pulled him back. He pushed the man towards the exit.

"Sorry for that ladies. We have certain policies. No means no." The guard winked at Sasha and went about kicking the guy out. Giselle looked at her friend.

"I was having doubts just now, but it looks like this place is seriously legit."

"Were you seriously about to punch him in the face?" Sasha laughed. Giselle made a muscle. n

"I've learned enough moves in my kick boxing class," she said.

"Maybe I oughta take those classes with you," Sasha suggested

"Stick to dancing babe. Let's go!" Giselle wiped her hands off and began dancing her way to the center of the club in front of the stage. Sasha trailed behind Giselle. She kept her eyes out on all the dancers to see if she would fit in herself. So far, none of the women had anything she didn't have.

"Jeez, Giselle you oughta be doing their makeup," Sasha muttered. "They could seriously use it. And their hair."

"Quit it," Giselle said. "You not supposed to be talking shit." They found a good spot in the center to get a good view of the stage. When the strippers started dancing both the men and the woman in the place began cheering their heads off and of course throwing money.

Giselle noticed another woman who was dressed just as scantily as the other dancers but she wasn't dancing. She was directing traffic between the dancers with a clipboard in her hand.

"Hey look, she might be the one we can talk to about the openings!" Giselle shouted at Sasha. "Are you sure you wanna try this out?" Sasha nodded at her in confirmation.

"Alright let's go!"

"Hey, excuse me," Giselle called to the woman. She turned around and frowned at them.

"Can I help you?" She asked.

"We were wondering about the openings," Sasha said. "There's word going on that the club is looking for dancers." Giselle was proud of Sasha for wanting to go through with this. However, just staring at this woman in front of them, Giselle was downright intimidated. The woman was tall and curvy with a pair of boobs someone probably paid a pretty penny for. She was radiant with light skin that glowed. Giselle was exactly the opposite of her. But that's why it was Sasha going for the job and not Giselle. She was in no comparison to the beautiful women walking around here.

The woman looked them up and down slowly. Then out of nowhere, she cut her eyes and frowned.

"Sorry but no thanks," she said.

"No thanks?" Sasha asked crossing her arms.

"You don't have the right look," she said.

"How about we talk to someone in charge," Giselle said.

"I am in charge. The owner of the club gave me the strict responsibility to choose girls. And I'm not interested in either of you so...buh bye." Both Giselle and Sasha just stood with their mouths open not believing how they were just dismissed.

"Let's just go," Giselle said. "Fuck her."

"Well if we're gonna leave, we gonna leave in style. I know I got more than the right look."

"So what you want to do?" Giselle asked.

"What I do best," Sasha winked.

*Chapter Five*

"Is that all you need Reign?" Reign looked at Charlotte and took a sip of the drink she had brought up for him. 'Is that all you need Reign' was a nice way of asking if he wanted her to suck his dick. Why was it that all these females kept suggesting he put his dick in their mouths?

"I think the better question is what you think you should give me?" Reign said to her. She smiled seductively.

"If you tell Khloe not to interrupt, I can give you a lot." Reign stood from his chair. He could see her tense up as he walked in a circle around her.

"Tell me what it is that you will give me Charlotte," he ordered softly. She looked around at him as he circled her.

"Well for starters I can take your whole dick into my mouth until you're balls deep, and you know I am very flexible. I'll ride you so good you'll lose you're fucking mind." Reign stopped pacing around her. What she said obviously sounded good, but truly he just wasn't turned on. He went to his chair and plopped down.

"I think I'll pass," he said. She opened her mouth to say something but then closed it. She sauntered over to his desk and came behind it. Reign just watched her as she pushed his chair back and straddled him.

"Are you sure?" she asked. She took his hands and placed each on her ass.

"Very sure," he answered. She pouted, but just before she could get up, his office door burst open. She jumped up, falling over as she tripped in her hurry. When she stood and looked, Khloe was at the door gawking at them. Reign still stayed sitting casually as Charlotte tripped and ran out of the room. Khloe glared after her but said nothing. She slammed the door shut once Charlotte was gone.

"What the fuck do you think you're doing?" She snapped.

"She was inviting me into her body I guess."

"This is the bullshit I'm talking about Reign. Every time I turn my fucking back you got another girl in here worshipping your dick! I'm not gonna put up with this shit no more you hear me?!" Reign just stared at her.

"Hello I am talking to you! You hear what the fuck I'm saying," she exclaimed. Reign looked at her for a long moment before he finally spoke in his normal calm tone.

"I hear you, I'm just tryna figure out who the hell you think you are. Cause ya damn sure ain't my wife." Khloe crossed her arms in denial about his words.

"So for now," Reign continued. "Get the fuck out my office and come back when you figure out how you can and cannot talk to me." Khloe stomped her foot.

"I'm sorry okay. But I hate it when those girls come in here like that." Reign just shrugged.

"I don't care what you hate Khloe, watch your fucking mouth when you talk to me." The intercom in his office made static before one of his guards spoke.

"I think you should pull up the video for the main room," he said.

"What's going on?" Reign asked back into the intercom.

"Pretty interesting entertainment. And it ain't from one of your girls." Reign stood from his desk went over to the corner of his large office where he had a computer set up. He hardly ever watched what happened in his club while the party was going on, but sometimes he kept watch through the cameras when the guards needed him to see something.

He turned on the computer and connected the camera in the main room. To his amazement, there was a tall, dark skinned beauty dancing on one of the center poles that the girls used when they weren't on stage. Both men and women were surrounding her, cheering her on as she twirled along the pole. When her feet hit the ground after her twirling, she held onto the pole and lifted herself up, spreading her legs in a split. She danced to the rhythm of the music. Reign saw every girl dance before he hired them, and so far this woman was the most stylistically talented that he'd ever seen.

"Do you see her?" the guard asked.

"Oh I see her," Reign replied. "Thanks for the heads up."

"I told that wannabe to leave," Khloe huffed.

"You mean you spoke with her?" Reign asked.

"Yeah. She wanted to know about the openings but I told her you wouldn't be interested and she didn't have the look. But apparently she didn't understand what the hell I meant."

"Yeah, I don't quite understand myself. Go down there and give her my card and set up a meeting between us."

"But Reign, she's-"

"Do what I said Khloe." He ordered. "And this is coming from your boss, not your fuck buddy." She crossed her arms and huffed.

"Okay Reign." She nodded and left the office. Reign shook his head and sat back down. Sometimes he wondered why he even bothered to deal with Khloe.

She had tendencies that he really didn't like. Yet still though, he always went back to her. Taking a deep breath he left his office to take a small walk outside to clear his mind.

********

Khloe walked angrily back into the main area of the club. The woman had finished dancing as people kept shoving money in her hands. After she accepted all the money, she walked away with her short friend she had with her earlier. Khloe found them.

"Guess what," Khloe said dryly. They both just looked at her. She handed the woman Reign's card. "Guess my boss does think you're interesting."

"Would you look at that," she smiled.

"What's your name?" Khloe asked her.

"Sasha, my name is Sasha." Khloe wrote her name down on the clipboard she was holding.

"Come back tomorrow around 3pm. You'll be meeting with the boss then." Sasha nodded and smiled.

"I think you owe me an apology now," Sasha said. "After all, you were wrong all along about me." Khloe sucked her teeth.

"You ain't getting shit from me. But I'll take that money now," she said holding out her hand.

"No, that's Sasha's money," the small woman spoke up.

"Ain't no one talking to you little girl." Giselle just stared at her as she continued to talk to Sasha.

"You're not a licensed dancer with us and you cannot collect money from our customers. So that money you collected belongs to the club." Khloe just held out her hand.

"Just give it to her," Giselle said. "You still got that interview tomorrow." Sasha handed over the money forcefully.

"Are you a dancer?" Sasha asked her.

"Sometimes. But I'm the owner's assistant and girlfriend. So basically I'm in charge around here."

"No wonder you're such a bitch!" Sasha said delightfully. "No matter, thanks for the card. Me and my home girl have men dying to buy us drinks. Later." Now it was Khloe's turn to be shocked at their dismissal. Giselle couldn't help but laugh as they stood in front of the crowded bar.

"I can tell you right now me and that hoe ain't gonna get along," Sasha said.

"Don't worry about her. She just mad you're already better than her. Lemme buy you a drink this time," Giselle offered.

While Giselle was prepared to buy as many drinks as she wanted for the both of them, they didn't really get a chance. Men were all around prepared to buy them any drink they needed.

Giselle felt her phone vibrating. When she looked it was Dean calling her. She rolled her eyes and ignored the call. Tucking the phone back into her shorts pocket she focused on the man next to Sasha to make sure he wasn't going to do anything slick. Her phone began to buzz in short bursts which let her know she was receiving text messages.

"Who's blowing up your phone?" Sasha asked her, when Giselle looked at her phone again.

"Mr. one minute," Giselle said. Sasha just shrugged at laughed at her. She looked at her messages. He's sent her five straight messages. *Where are you? Call me back NOW. I just went back to your place and you're not home. We need to talk about what happened earlier. I don't appreciate you ignoring my call either Giselle, so looks like there's a lesson you'll be learning soon.*

If Giselle didn't know his dick game was whack she would have been turned on by his forcefulness. She liked when a man took charge, and maybe Dean was able to take charge with his attitude and words, but he sure as hell couldn't take charge with his body or actions. But even though she wasn't even in the mood for him especially after having to kick the fucker out her house because he couldn't satisfy her she decided to call him.

"I'll be back," Giselle said, patting Sasha on the shoulder. Sasha nodded and returned to her male company. Giselle went towards the back of the club where she could find the bathroom in hopes that it was quiet enough. The bathroom line was long with women, so she walked passed it to a separate hall that seemed empty. There was only one door in the hall with an exit sign over it, but no one was coming and going. When she dialed Dean, he picked up on the first ring.

"Hello," she greeted casually.

"Where you at?" He asked roughly.

"I'm chillin with Sasha."

"Where at Giselle?"

"Why does it matter Dean?' She asked. "I dismissed you earlier for a reason."

"Look, I don't know who the hell you think you dealing with, but I'm not one of those little ass niggas. I left to give you some time but you aint gonna be ignoring me and shit. So where are you?"

"I'm chillin with my home girl Dean, I don't need no man hovering over my shoulder right now. So how bout we try all this shit tomorrow?"

"You know what, I know you with another man."

"Excuse me?! Who the fuck do you think you are? And if I'm with another man, so the fuck what?"

"So is that what we doing? You fuck me then go fuck someone else? I ain't enough for you?" Giselle was beyond shocked. Was this man serious? He honestly thought he was putting a dent in her pussy when they had sex? That she was supposed to fall in love with him?

"Fuck off Dean." She hung up the phone. She didn't have to justify where she was or prove to him that she wasn't with another man at the moment. None of that shit mattered. What mattered was that he thought he deserved her full attention anyway. If she was a different kind of woman then damn right she would be getting fucked by another man, and she would be getting fucked good as a matter of fact. Her phone went off in her hand again. She quickly silenced it.

"You done lost your fucking mind," she said to herself speaking of Dean. She turned to walk back towards the main room.

"I don't know what woman told you that you was all a that." She looked down at her phone in time to see he was calling again.

"Like I said, fuck off," she said to herself once more, deciding to turn the phone off completely. She was so caught up in herself that she didn't see or hear a door in the hall open. She kept marching along to go and tell Sasha what the hell this man just said to her, when she was stopped in her tracks by a hard body. She squeaked in surprise. Instead of landing on her ass from the impact, strong hands grabbed onto her arms to keep her upright. Looking straight forward all she saw was a broad chest. She inclined her head and looked up for what seemed like minutes before she actually saw the face of the person holding her.

"Sorry sweetheart," he said. His deep voice vibrated through her skin and into her bones. Even though his voice was deep, his tone was very soft and caring. His muscles were subtle under his shirt, but Giselle could still see them. All she could think about at the moment was draping herself over his broad chest. She looked at his face. He had a neat goatee that framed his plump lips, but that wasn't w5hat caught her complete attention. His hairline was trimmed to perfection that led to his stunning neat dreads. Giselle's mouth was shaped in an 'o' as she just looked at this specimen of a man. And she thought Dean was perfection. No, this man in front of her was perfection. Both her eyes and her lady parts agreed with each other.

Reign was in awe. So much so that he couldn't manage to take his eyes off the small female he was still holding onto. She was so petite he felt like a giant next to her. She was just pushing maybe 5'3 compared to his 6'0 stature. While she was short, she was still definitely all woman. Her skin was soft under his hands, making Reign want to caress her completely. Her body was perfectly proportioned. Her breasts were nice and round and just the right size to fit into his hands. Her hips curved graciously and all he could think about was how soft her curves would be. Even though it was hot in the club from all the dancing bodies, her cinnamon skin was radiant and fresh. With long messy curls, she almost seemed childlike, but there was a spark in her eyes. When she smiled at him, he nearly lost his cool. Man, if angels ever walked the earth, they'd probably look like this woman right here. Reign cleared his throat and actually spoke to her.

"You good?" he asked her.

"Yeah, yeah I'm good," she said quietly. He let her go and Giselle ached at the loss.

"You were cursing up a storm little lady," he said. "Who got on your bad side?" Giselle scoffed.

"Men! Always walking around here thinking cause ya'll have a dick you can do and say whatever the fuck you want to." He smiled brightly showing off his perfect teeth.

"Not all of us," he laughed. "But I mean, we're humans. We're allowed to be stupid."

"To an extent," Giselle smiled. "But um, sorry for bumping into you." Giselle tried to keep her cool as he looked down at her. The stare of his soft brown eyes was a caress on her heated skin. Giselle didn't know if it was the height difference, or maybe it was just the raw power he gave off as a man, but she felt like an ant in front of him and intimidation didn't even seem the right word to describe how she was feeling.

"I uh...gonna go now." She stammered. She went to back away from him. And like someone in the universe was playing a joke on her, she tripped on her feet. Again, if he hadn't reached out to catch her, she would have fell on her butt.

"Been drinking?" He teased. She gave him a

guilty smile as she tried not to feel embarrassed. He set her right and held onto her for a little bit. His hands were large against her arms. She was beginning to imagine what his hands would feel like all over her body. She didn't know if it was a good thing or a bad thing to be daydreaming about such a sexy ass man. Truth be told it was probably the last time she would see him again so it didn't matter what she daydreamed about.

"Just a couple drinks," she answered softly. "I'm a big girl though, I can handle it."

"I don't doubt that. Just don't go tripping again."

"I won't," she answered. When he let her go again, she kept herself from telling him to put his hands back on her. Clearing her throat she backed away without tripping this time. He smiled at her as she moved out of his way and walked back to the main club. Forget telling Sasha about Dean's trifflin' ass. She needed to tell her friend about the man that just lit her damn skin on fire.

Reign couldn't help watching the mystery

woman's ass as she walked off. She was wearing shorts that fit snugly on her. It was then that he noticed she was wearing a halter top. The left side of her back was tattooed with a rose vine. It traveled from her shoulder and down her back but her top hid where the tattoo stopped.

"I think I like women with ink," he said to himself, watching her plump bottom march away. He shook his head at himself. He didn't exactly know where that thought came from but the ink on that little lady was an added turn on. Reign was surrounded by half naked women all day. But here, a small woman wearing a reasonable amount of clothing had his full attention. Until now, Reign couldn't remember a time where he ever looked that long at a female or even looked at them twice.

"Fuck it," he said to himself going to follow her. When was he truly going to see this beauty again? He had to at least know her name. Just as he rounded the corner, Khloe popped up in his face. She was talking about the girl he wanted to interview but Reign wasn't paying attention.

"Yeah, yeah okay Khloe. Just wait a sec," he said hushing her up. He moved her out of the way and went into the main room. Only when he looked around, that little beauty was nowhere to be found.

********

Giselle dragged Sasha out of the club by her arm. When they got outside, Sasha tore her arm away.

"The hell is your problem?" Sasha asked.

"Dean was talking to me all types of crazy when I called him." Giselle said.

"Okay so what, you wanna roll up on him or something and kick his ass?" Giselle rolled her eyes. Her best friend swore she was some sort of gangsta.

"Of course not Sasha."

"You took those kick boxing classes for nothing then if you don't wanna kick someone's ass sometime."

"Look, this ain't about Dean. I'm just saying that as I hung up on his arrogant ass I turned around and bumped into the sexiest man I've ever seen in my life. And seriously Sasha, I mean that literally. Sexiest. Man. Ever." Giselle reported. Sasha gasped.

"So what the fuck we doing out here?!" She snapped. "Get back in there and let's find him again. What did you say to him when you bumped into him?"

"Nothing much really, and it's all a blur anyway. I couldn't concentrate on anything but  just looking as his sexy ass. He's tall as fuck but he was gentle when he held me and his voice was the right amount of baritone and softness mixed together. Lord help me he was so fucking fine. I didn't even get a chance to ask him his name" Sasha gazed at her friend in awe. She'd never seen Giselle that taken away by a man. Not even Dean. She knew Giselle was shy when meeting new people but Sasha wasn't going to let her friend squander this opportunity.

"Come on," Sasha said taking her arm. "We gotta find him again. We can't let a man who's got you this would up get away." This time it was Sasha dragging Giselle back into the club. Giselle was immediately nervous. How could a sexy man like that even be interested in knowing her name much less wanting to talk to her again. However, with Sasha on this mission to finding him with her, Giselle wasn't going to get out of confronting him again.

"Do you see him?" Sasha asked. Giselle looked all over the club. She didn't spot him.

"Follow me," Giselle shouted. She didn't know what he was doing in the hall in the first place but maybe he was still there. They rounded the corner to the hall in a hurry, but it was empty. Sasha cursed to herself. Giselle was equally disappointed. The sexiest man she'd ever seen and she let him slip away without even knowing who he was. Now he was nowhere to be found.

"He's gone," Giselle said.

She needed a strong batch of coffee. Rolling out of bed, Giselle got tied up in the bed sheets. She cursed and tried to get herself loose, but she rolled out of the bed and fell to the ground. When she sat up she had to hold her temple to ease the aching.

"What time is it?" She asked no one in particular. Looking at her alarm clock. It was just after ten. Then she remembered that Sasha had her meeting today with the strip club. Getting up slowly, Giselle grabbed her cell phone from the night table and stumbled downstairs to get some coffee going.

"Wake up sleepy head," she said into the phone when Sasha picked up. Sasha groaned.

"What do you want?" She asked.

"You have your meeting today. And if I know any better you're just as hung over as I am. So ya gotta get up and get yourself together now." Sasha grunted again.

"Fine! Make me some coffee," Sasha groaned.

"Got it covered."

"Be there soon." When she hung up the phone, Giselle poured more coffee into the coffeemaker. Since she had an appetite and she knew Sasha was going to have an appetite as well, she picked out ingredients to make pancakes, bacon, and eggs. By the time she placed her fourth pancake in the pan her doorbell rang. Sasha was leaning against the doorway in jeans shorts and a t-shirt. Her soft black hair was matted and all over the place. She was wearing large sunglasses that covered most of her face. Giselle opened the door wider to let her in. She immediately went to the kitchen and plopped down at the table.

"You look like shit," Giselle teased.

"Tell me about it," she said. Giselle poured her a large cup of coffee. Sasha began sipping immediately.

"It's so good," she groaned.

"Good old Folgers." When Giselle finished cooking she sat down across from Sasha and they both began to eat.

"Are you excited about the meeting?" Giselle asked. Sasha only shrugged.

"I'm a little bit worried. I mean, what if I'm in over my head? Last night I was drunk the whole time. Do you think it was even smart to try and do this whole thing?"

"Are you kidding? Don't you remember how many men and women were all over you while you danced? You were fucking hot!"

"And do you think the boss is gonna think that? I don't think I'm that exciting when I'm sober," she said somberly.

"Trust me Sasha, he's gonna love you. You're gorgeous. None of those women in there had a look like yours!" Giselle was being honest. Her best friend was as tall as Naomi Campbell and dark just like her. Her long straight hair was flawless when she was on point and Giselle knew for a fact that her friend would have no problem being the life of the party, sober or not.

"Well I was thinking..." Sasha said. "That you

should come with me."

"Of course I'll come for support."

"No I meant, that you should come and get a job too," Sasha looked at Giselle through her large sunglasses.

"Oh hell no!" Giselle exclaimed "Are you forgetting who I am? There's no way I even have the confidence to pull off an exotic routine. And I sure as hell cannot go stand in front of people and do it either. Nope. No way." Sasha began laughing.

"When we dance together. You keep up well with me. I teach you everything I know and you do it perfectly!"

"I like to dance Sasha. But behind closed doors. So let's talk about you now. What are you going to wear?" Sasha snickered but dropped the subject.

"I bought some things for you to choose from." Giselle noticed the large bag she had been carrying.

"Now that I can do. Let's go-" The doorbell rang interrupting her. Giselle and Sasha looked at each other. Giselle wasn't expecting anyone.

"Well go answer it!" Sasha ordered. Giselle

stood and tied her robe shut and went to the door. When she opened it, a full bouquet of flowers was being shoved in her face.

"What you want Dean?" Giselle asked, putting a hand on her hip. He looked at her from over the flowers.

"To apologize. I realize that I may have been a dick to you."

"You may have?" Giselle questioned.

"Okay fine, I was a dick to you. But you gotta understand that my mind was in another place and when I get upset, I can't really control myself."

"Well that's too bad isn't it?"

"Oh come on Giselle don't be stubborn. I'm apologizing. Take the flowers baby, please." Giselle tried to retain her hard look, but his soft expression did her in.

"Fine, apology accepted," Giselle grunted.

"Can I come in?" He asked. Giselle hesitated for a moment.

"Sasha is here."

"No matter, I don't mind." Not wanting to be a

bitch she nodded and let him inside.

"Hi Sasha," he greeted. She waved at him since her mouth was full of bacon.

"Here, sit down. I have more food left." When he sat around the table, she piled another plate with food and sat it in front of him. She placed the flower and vase on her window sill to soak up some sun.

"Those flowers are gorgeous," Sasha said, washing down her food with the coffee.

"Yes, I know Giselle loves flowers so I figured I'd hook her up with some," he said. That was true. Giselle did love flowers.

"Well that's his way of apologizing after he was being a dick last night," Giselle scoffed.

"Oh yeah, I heard about that," Sasha said. "Honestly Dean, I would be careful. Giselle took a kickboxing class and even though she is small, she'd probably kick your ass." All three of them laughed.

"Don't worry I will keep that in mind," he said.

"Anyway, me and Sasha got something to do. Entertain yourself until I'm done," Giselle said. He nodded as he enjoyed his breakfast and coffee. Giselle took Sasha by the hand and led her up to the bedroom.

"Look at you," Sasha smiled. "You got a full grown man eating the food you cooked in your kitchen. Looks like you bout to be hitched real soon."

"Oh do not say that," Giselle said. "Next thing you know, he's really about to try and be with me. Right now, we just fuck okay? I like Dean, but…well you know what the problem is."

"I guess you right boo, but do you even plan on settling down anytime soon? So what if Dean sucks in bed, his sperm still works." Giselle's mouth fell open.

"What are you saying? What are you really saying right now Sasha?"

"Look, we been best friends since we both beat up that punk Henry in the 4th grade," she smiled. "We're both almost thirty. The maternity clock is ticking. And well, we all know I don't have a man, and I ain't close to having a man. But you…you got someone. Aren't you thinking about having a family?" Giselle played with the string of her robe.

"No I'm not thinking about a family Sasha. I mean, I got you," Giselle sighed.

"Yeah but that's different. I know you want a baby," Sasha told her.

"It's not like I've thought about it before but...I guess if I fell in love then maybe." Some women had that natural desire to be a mother, but Giselle didn't have that. What she did feel was that if she was with a man that she loved and he wanted children, she'd have no problem giving him what he wanted. For now it seemed that love wasn't in her future. She couldn't even find a man that satisfied her mentally and physically.

"Dean might make a good daddy," Sasha teased. Giselle slapped her friend playfully. She was sure Dean would be a great father, and a great man but she just wasn't ready to commit. Maybe the hard reality would be that she would probably end up happy with Dean emotionally, but unhappy with him sexually. Sometimes you just had to make sacrifices.

"Yeah he might. I'll be with him one day, but I'll probably have so many dildo's I can start up my own adult store," Giselle joked.

"Don't worry about that. Just get yourself some

orgasms before you seal the deal with Dean." Giselle's mind instantly flashed to the mystery man she bumped into last night. He was truly a divine specimen. She didn't quite know why but she imagined he was more than just good in bed. Then that's what she thought of Dean and it backfired against her tremendously. Giselle couldn't shake the look of his brown eyes out of her head. Not only his brown eyes, but his plump lips, his big hands. It all made Giselle shiver. Too bad she wasn't about to see that man again.

"Come on, your hair looks a hot ass mess," Giselle said shaking herself from her deep thoughts and getting down to business with getting Sasha ready for her meeting.

********

Reign's eyes blinked open. He looked straight up at his ceiling. The sun was coming through the patio doors in his bedroom, bathing the room in warmth. He blinked and rolled over, landing on the emptiness on the other side of his king size bed. He yawned and stretched but stayed laying down as he looked out of his patio doors at the bright blue sky. He loved where he lived near the beach. It wasn't too close to the waters but when he opened his windows early in the morning he could smell the saltiness of the sea draft through his home. But the main reason he loved his home was because it was away from the noise of the city.

The noise was one thing, but Reign liked his space. He liked to be alone. It was ironic since he worked at the busiest and loudest club in the city, but that just gave him more of a reason to want his own space away from all of that. Ever since Reign could remember, he always liked his personal space. As he continued to age however, he was beginning to realize that waking up alone depressed him more and more as each day went by. Reign had thought about inviting Khloe over, but at the last minute he'd always change his mind. For some reason, keeping his space to himself gave him peace of mind. The last thing he ever wanted was his space to be violated. So instead, Reign bought Khloe a nice little home where he spent some nights there with her. He enjoyed being with her, but he had his limits. It made him wonder on how it would be once he did allow her to move in. Maybe he'd have to have a serious talk with her about her attitude. If she was indeed going to bear his children, he wasn't going to keep her in a separate home. Again, ironic how he loved his space but he was thinking about moving a woman in with him and adding children to the equation. But he had his reasons. *You'd better give me grandkids. I don't care if I'm alive or not.* He smiled as he thought about the last words his mother said to him. Even on her deathbed she was giving him orders. He didn't think he would want a family once she handed him the keys to the strip club.

Somehow though, his mother definitely had found a way to have a family. Especially as she had started out as a broke woman, dancing on poles to feed herself and her child, and ended up as the owner of her own club. Reign as a child never understood where his mother went when she dressed in her skimpy outfits, but when he turned 16 he followed her one night and saw just what she was doing. He was angry at her at first. It took him learning the harsh reality that he was cared for with the money his mother had earned doing what she had to do. He was humbled when he realized the money she made dancing was what bought him the clothes on his back, the shoes on his feet, and the food in his stomach. He learned to appreciate the things that people did just to survive. That's why he could never talk down to a woman simply because she stripped. Since then he put his mother on a pedestal and was there for her whenever she needed him to be. And true, she was gone but he wanted to fulfil her wish to see him with his own children.

Sighing, he sat up in bed. Reaching for his phone on the night table stand, he leaned back against the headboard of his bed to check his messages. There were emails from his vendors that he ordered equipment and supplies for the club and a message from Khloe reminding him about the meeting with the dancer. When he looked at his watch, it was noon and time for him to finally get out of bed. Just as he used the bathroom his phone rang.

"Yes, Khloe?" He asked when he picked up the phone.

"Are you still home?" She asked.

"Yes. What's the matter?" He knew there was

something she wanted to ask for.

"I just wanted a little time with you before we went into the club," she finally said.

"Sorry K, you'll just have to wait until later," he told her.

"It wouldn't be a problem if you actually let me come over and stay at your place sometimes," she mumbled. Reign rolled his eyes. He knew this was coming.

"Khloe I fucked you yesterday, why you bothering me?" He asked. "Do I not satisfy you enough?"

"Stop it Reign! You know damn well you be having my pussy aching, but when it's so good I just want some more. I can't get enough."

"So hold onto that appetite girl and just wait for me to get to the club. I'll take care of it."

"Okay fine sexy, see you later." Reign hung up the phone. Shaking his head he went down to his large kitchen to find something to eat before he showered and dressed to get to the club.

Instead of driving to the club today, Reign decided to ride his motorcycle into town. He hadn't rode his bike in a while and he could use the fresh air. With his bike he reached the club in 30 minutes. When he pulled his bike up to the club he saw a line of women already outside.

"What in the world," he muttered. He quickly pulled his bike into the parking lot and parked it in his space. He used the side entrance to enter the club. The moment he walked through the door, he had a flashback of the little beauty he'd bumped into back here. He recalled the way she felt when she bumped into him. She was so small in his hands and seemed so delicate but he had a feeling that under all of that she was so much more. He wanted to run his hands through her hair, he wanted to caress her soft skin, and he wanted to kiss her soft lips. He was so much taller than her that he would have to bend over to kiss her because there was no way she was going to reach his lips otherwise. He imagined himself picking her up easily and her wrapping her legs around him as they kissed. He could hold her so firmly and perfect in his arms to fuck her while standing up. Reign shivered as he felt arousal ride his body. The thought of a woman never aroused him anymore and here he was with a stiffy in his jeans. He tried to push down his arousal as he walked further into the club. He went straight to his office and took off his motorcycle vest and put down his helmet.

"Khloe come here," he spoke into the intercom, directing it to the ladies dressing room. No one answered but within five minutes his office opened and Khloe walked in. She was still wearing jeans and a bustier.

"Who are all those girls out front?" He asked her.

"The girls I brought in for you to take a look at, see if they fit for the openings. That was my job." Reign nodded.

"I suppose you're right. Why you got jeans on?" He asked. He was still stiff in his jeans and was hoping to relieve himself.

"I was organizing things with the new girls so you can see them. So I just dressed regular." Reign huffed and undid the buckle to his belt and unsnapped his jeans. When she saw his aching boner, he didn't have to tell her what he wanted her to do with it.

"You must miss me too. Look at how you're worked up," she cooed at him. If only she knew that Reign was like this because of the memory of another woman.

Khloe came to him and pushed him to sit down. Plopping down on her knees she gripped the base of his penis and shoved it into her mouth. He gripped her hair tightly to control her movements on his shaft. Khloe wasn't bad at giving him oral sex, but sometimes he had to reel her in a little bit. He winced as she dragged her teeth along his shaft. He kept telling her it didn't feel good when she used her teeth but she insisted that he loved it. Rolling his eyes, he just let her do what she wanted and when she finally got a rhythm, he would be able to enjoy her mouth. As she continued to bite him annoyingly, he looked at his watch. He knew security would be paging for him soon especially with all those women waiting. Khloe began slobbering all over him and making gagging sounds even though she didn't even have half of him in her mouth. There was no time for this shit. He pulled her by the hair lightly, taking her off his penis.

"What are you doing?" He asked her. She looked at him with a blank stare.

"What do you mean? I-I'm sucking you off."

"No, you're not Khloe. You're just spitting on me." She continued to just stare. "You're not a porn star Khloe, stop trying to act like one. Just suck it. It's so simple." She huffed and shoved his dick back in her mouth. This time, she deep throated as much as she could and sucked him simply, hollowing out her cheeks.

"Perfect Khloe," he egged her on. She moaned around his shaft amplifying his pleasure. He held her head still and fucked her mouth. Closing his eyes was a dangerous thing. Behind his closed lids he saw that little beauty on her knees instead of Khloe, using her small dainty mouth to suck him off. He imagined her wild curls bouncing all over the place as her head bobbed up and down. He grunted as his release spurted into her mouth. When he opened his eyes, he was disappointed at the fact that everything was a fantasy. There was no little beauty sucking him off. When Khloe smiled at him, that's when he felt like a dick for imagining another woman while she was giving him her all. That little beauty was only a one time encounter and he didn't think he would be seeing her again. She was a fantasy in his head. Khloe was real, and Khloe was who he had.

He picked her up from the floor. Dragging her jeans down roughly, he sat her on the desk and spread her legs. He shoved two fingers inside her wet pussy and stroked her slowly. She let her head fall back as she moaned. Wasting no time, he curled his fingers inside her and stroked her at a fast pace. Her eyes rolled upwards as he continued to stimulate her G-spot.

"Do not squirt on me," he ordered. "We don't have the time to clean up a squirt." She nodded but never looked at him. Her toes curled and her legs shook. He felt her insides grip his fingers as she came hard. Her hips jacked up from the desk as she rode out the orgasm. The moment he pulled his fingers from her the intercom in his office went off.

"Ready for me to send the girls up?" Khloe and Reign looked at each other and smirked.

"I'm ready in 5," Reign answered. He helped Khloe stand and they both went into the bathroom to clean up.

"I'll take you for lunch later," he told her when they finished. He opened the door for her to leave.

"I thought I would be in the meetings with you. After all, I kinda am your assistant and I know the girls we already have. I can tell which one of these new girls will fit in, and which ones will just be trouble." Reign hadn't thought about that. He nodded and closed the door.

"Fine. But while we speak I don't want you interrupting us, and I don't want you saying unnecessary things. The moment you do I'll put you out."

"I won't," she said. He nodded and sent word down that he was ready for the women to come upstairs.

*******

Sasha hadn't been this nervous since the night

she lost her virginity. Now here she was standing in a long line of girls waiting to meet with the owner of the club. She didn't expect there to be this many females but that was her own fault. Everyone knew this strip club was one of the best to work at because it was the most popular. She was grateful she even got the chance, but now she wasn't so sure she could beat out all these other chicks.

"Don't worry. They won't make the cut," Giselle said at her side.

"When did you become the expert?" Sasha joked.

"Just look at them. Their makeup is a hot mess and their outfits aren't cute. You look the part."

"Giselle, I have on the most clothes here! If I would have known, I could have dressed more appropriately." The both of them had decided it would be better if she wore something normal, like the tank top and high waist jean shorts with wedge heels she was wearing now. They were convinced it would give Sasha the edge on the other girls. What if she didn't even get the chance to change to convince him to hire her? The rest of the females were dressed in their best skimpy outfits. Sasha felt completely out of place.

"Stick with the plan alright, and don't chicken out," Giselle told her confidently. Sasha found comfort in her friend's words.

"Still don't think you should be interviewed too?" Sasha asked her.

"I told you no. I am not a dancer in front of a crowd. You do ya thing girl." Sasha knew Giselle would be a perfect dancer. She was the epitome of a perfect human. She was good at every damn thing and it wasn't because she practiced or tried too much. She was just gifted in that way. She did yoga, she was active at the gym, she took kickboxing, she danced, she cooked, and was a beautician, and a stylist. And for all those things, Giselle didn't struggle to get the hand of it. She was just good at it. But while she was naturally gifted, Sasha felt that she did all those things, and looked for more things to do simply because she too was alone. However, instead of trying to fill that nothingness with someone, she just filled it with all these activities. None of those things however would keep her friend company at night though.

"I bet imma get you to dance for the owner," Sasha teased.

"Oh hell no, please don't do nothing stupid and ruin your shot at working here."

"But how fabulous would it be if we worked here together. We can be a duo every night and every man in this joint is going to want a dance from us!"

"Sounds delightful, but still no." Sasha was only teasing her friend. She wasn't going to make her try and be a dancer here, she was however definitely going to try to get her friend to work at the club. What better place for a beautician than a high end strip club whose strippers clearly needed lessons on makeup and beauty.

"Alright girls, come in," the security guard ordered. He opened the front doors and let everyone in. Another guard led the girls to the main room where they were to wait to be called to see the owner. Now, it seemed to be getting real. She loved auditioning for regular dance gigs, but this was different. Exotic dancing was nothing to be taken lightly. And if you weren't good at it, you just weren't good at it.

"Wait, you notice that these meetings are going by fast?" Sasha asked, after the 4th girl came from the back of the building. She huffed in anger as she marched out of the club. Only 15 minutes has gone by and the 5th woman was already being lead to the back.

"Isn't that a good thing? It means we won't be here all day," Giselle shrugged.

"No, it means the owner is mean as fuck and he's dismissing girls quickly."

"You're overreacting," Giselle said. "Relax."

"Fuck this!" The 5th woman snapped, entering the main room again. She marched right to the exit and left. Sasha and Giselle looked at her with wide eyes.

"That woman just went in there 2 minutes ago," Sasha gasped.

"Yeah maybe he's mean as fuck," Giselle said. Sasha cut her eye at her friend. "Don't fret Sash. Damn, and I thought I was the shy one." Sasha made a face but hid her worries as they continued to wait. Within another 20 minutes, it was their turn to go up.

"One at a...time," the guard said slowly as he locked eyes with Sasha. She felt her cheeks heat up under his stare. Looking everywhere but him she answered.

"We're a duo," she said. "So we should interview together right?"

"Um, yeah sure," he answered. His eyes wandered all over her. She was a goddess of a female, a beauty he'd never seen before in his life. A small smile curved her lips as her friend ushered her towards the back of the club, breaking their stares. Dalen Knead had seen enough naked women in his time working here, and none of them looked as good as that chocolate martini of a woman.

"I saw the way he was checking you out!" Giselle teased, elbowing her friend.

"He wasn't checking me out," Sasha blushed, knowing damn well he was most definitely checking her out.

"Yeah and I saw the way you were looking at him too." What wasn't there to look at? He was tall. He had mysterious dark eyes. His body was in impeccable shape. So yes, maybe Sasha was looking at him.

"That's an ocean I definitely want to take a dip in," Sasha said.

"After you get this job maybe you should get his number," Giselle said. "I tell ya, once you see a man that makes you think twice about them, then I suggest you not make the opportunity pass you by."

"Yeah just like you did last night with that sexy man you found. You was running out to me instead of getting that man's number." Giselle elbowed her friend again.

"Shut up about that," she smiled. "Now put your game face on and let's get you this job."


Reign sighed and leaned back in his chair. He looked over at Khloe who was taking notes.

"What in the hell is you writing?" he asked her. "We turned away every single female that came up in here." She looked at him and smiled brightly.

"Gotta make sure they don't try to come back again. So I gotta remember who they are." Something was up. Khloe knew exactly the type of women she needed to be bringing in here, and all of these damn women were not it. They were dressed horribly, out of shape, and left nothing for a man's imagination. They had poor etiquette and no charm to their personality.

"You think I'm stupid?" Reign asked her.

"What?" She tried to put on an innocent face.

"You know damn well I wasn't gonna hire none of those damn women. So why the hell would you even give them a chance to come sit in here?"

"How am I supposed to know who you would and wouldn't hire? These girls inquired about the position and I gave them the information. What else you wanted me to do?" Reign just rolled his eyes. If he had to go through the whole afternoon with these subpar women, he was going to lose his mind. Picking up his beer, he took a sip as the next woman knocked on his office door.

"Come in!" He shouted. The door creaked opened as if the woman behind it was afraid to come inside. Reign took another sip of his beer. A tall chocolate woman wearing a tank top and jean shorts entered the room. Already, Reign was interested.

"Come on," she whispered to someone still behind the door.

"No," they snapped.

"There's two of you?" Reign asked. The tall woman smiled at him.

"Yeah, but she's nervous," she replied.

"We are doing interviews one at a time," Khloe gritted. That little smile Khloe was wearing earlier was wiped completely off as she stared at the woman at the door.

"Yes true, but I thought we could just interview together. 2 bird's one stone," the woman said.

"That's if she ever comes inside," Reign added. He smiled at the tall woman. His smile made her let out a deep breath as if she was worried about something.

"Tell me about it," she said. "Get in here," she gritted behind the door. Reign took another sip of his drink. The tall woman yanked the person into the room and closed the door. Reign choked on his beer, sitting up straight as his eyes landed on his small beauty he was just fantasizing about.

Giselle was frozen. She didn't know what to do

or to say as her eyes connected with her mystery sexy man. She didn't even want to enter the room because she did not want Sasha to get her into this dancing thing. If her damn friend wasn't so persistent, Giselle would not have laid eyes on the man that she'd had lingering thoughts about. Nasty, dirty lingering thoughts at that. Now here she was staring at him again as he sat behind his large desk. It hit her then that he was the owner of the club.

"Welcome," he said easily and clearing his throat. Giselle nodded and looked away from him. She looked at Sasha who was smiling at him. Sasha took Giselle's arm and led her to the chairs, forcing her to sit in front of his desk. Even though she tried not to, every two seconds she was looking at him. It just so happens that whenever she looked at him, he was already looking at her. Now she was the nervous wreck. Giselle coughed at her friend. When Sasha looked at her, Giselle made subtle eye movements towards the man to get her to understand that he was the sexy man she'd met, but Sasha didn't have a clue as to what she was hinting.

"Shall we start with you?" he asked, looking at Sasha. She looked at him and nodded.

"My name is Sasha."

"Nice to meet you Sasha, my name is Reign." Giselle almost drooled. It was like he was born to be some kind of god.

"Hi Reign." Sasha greeted. Reign looked at his small beauty. She was just as timid as she was when he bumped into her but yet still, he was drawn to keep looking at her.

"So um, what is your experience?" Reign asked.

"Well, I don't have an exotic experience, but I am a-"

"Not qualified," Khloe snapped. "You need to have experience in this type of dancing."

"Be quiet, or get out," Reign said sternly. Giselle's eyes went wide at his voice of authority. Fuck he was sexy. Khloe sat back and crossed her arms.

"Anyway," Reign said. "Where do you dance?" He asked Sasha.

"I usually dance for companies, or I find shows to dance or choreograph. I've never really done exotic dancing in public until last night but I feel comfortable and I think I understand the art of seduction." Reign smiled at her. He liked this woman.

"Do you mind?" He asked, pointing to the empty space in the office, signaling he wanted her to dance for him.

"No I don't actually." Sasha stood and went to the empty space. While Reign was supposed to be looking at her, he stole a glance at the beauty looking at her friend. Just as Sasha started dancing he looked over at her. She was incredibly artistic and very flexible. She did several splits and acrobatic moves.

"Very nice," Reign said. When she sat back down she winked at her friend.

"So what do you aim to do here? Just dancing?" Reign asked her.

"Yes. I know you have private rooms for added entertainment. I can give special lap dances for any amount of time, but I don't intend to turn my dancing into sex," Sasha told him firmly.

"Then I don't think you can work here," Khloe piped up again. Reign slammed his hand on his desk and looked at her. All three women jumped. Khloe put her head down in silence. Reign glared at Khloe for a moment before turning his attention back to Sasha. He breathed in and let out his angered breath so he could continue talking with Sasha in a proper tone.

"That's fine if you don't want to have sex here Sasha. It's not something I would force you to do. You're more than what I expected today, and I will gladly like to give you a position. I, however need to be sure to protect the girls that already work here. I don't want to hire drama."

"I understand completely."

"So, you'll be under one month of probation. Don't feel offended if I have people looking out for you to make sure you're okay," he informed her. Sasha nodded.

"We just have a couple of base rules. Any money you make dancing is yours to keep. I profit from the amount of patrons that come through here and I don't cut you ladies a check so I see it fit you keep what you make. All the girls dance together at one point so make it your priority to learn the shared routines. You cannot bring anyone in here for free either. You're allowed to drink freely from the bar during your shifts but you are not to consume to the point of intoxication. That is an immediate termination. Fighting with the other girls will cost you a 150 dollars fine. Got it?'

"I got it, but just one more question. Are we allowed to have sex with employees?" Sasha asked.

"You're a grown woman, do as you wish," Reign smiled.

"Well good because your security guard downstairs is fine as hell." Reign couldn't help but laugh at her. Her friend only smiled but then elbowed Sasha.

"So now, what about you?" Reign asked, turning to his little beauty. She immediately stopped smiling.

"What about me?" She asked. Her voice was like a humming bird in his ears.

"You're here to be a dancer?" He asked. Instead of answering, she looked at Sasha who cleared her throat.

"Uh actually she's not a dancer," Sasha spoke up. Reign was confused.

"So how is it that I can help you little lady?" Giselle forced her cheeks not to heat. She couldn't speak for the fear of saying the things that was on her mind. And climbing over the desk and kissing him deeply was on her mind.

"You see," Sasha said. "I think she can offer me and the girls some things."

"And what the hell would that be?" Khloe asked. This time Reign didn't hush her.

"She's a beautician," Sasha said. Giselle realized then what her friend was trying to do. She would have been mad if a sexy ass man wasn't the owner of the club. Was it so bad for her to work where she could drool and daydream about him repeatedly?

"Want to explain more?" Reign asked her. Giselle smiled.

"I do makeup jobs and I style clothing. I know you're not looking for any of my talents but maybe we can work something out. From the way you sent all the previous women packing today shows you care about what your women look like." Reign never thought about what kind of makeup the women put on but every night before show time he had to tell at least one girl to change something about what she was wearing.

"I'll need to see what you got little lady," he said.

"I can show you what I got," she answered. Reign's dick woke up at those words. This was so not the right time to turn that sentence into something sexual.

"If I like it, I'd love to hire you," Reign told her.

"You don't want to know my rates?" She asked. He shrugged.

"I think I'm well off enough to handle it," he smiled.

"Reign!" Khloe snapped. "Are you seriously about to hire a makeup artist, that none of the girls are gonna use? Men come here to see them strip and dance, not pay attention to their makeup. It's a waste of money!"

"That is true," Giselle spoke up. "But that still don't mean he has to send girls out there looking like a clown. Last night some of the makeup jobs were horrible."

"You don't get to just come up in here and tell us how to run this business like you know what the fuck needs to be done," she snapped. Punching his desk, Reign rolled his chair over to Khloe. He took her by the elbow and pulled her towards him so he could whisper in her ear.

"I'm not gonna ask you again to shut up. Say one more word Khloe. I dare you." Khloe sat quiet. Reign would never put his hands on her, but that didn't mean he was a man to play with.

Although he had intended for only Khloe to hear it, both Sasha and Giselle heard the threat he passed to Khloe. His words and tone of voice silenced Khloe immediately and lit a flame in Giselle's underwear.

"Damn," Sasha whispered. Giselle elbowed her hard, already feeling protective of Reign for some reason. Reign turned back to the two women and cleared his throat.

"I'll take you up on any offer you have to help my club little lady. But as far as your makeup skills go, I'd love to see your work." Giselle just nodded.

"The both of you can come back tonight when

we're open. You can show me your skills little lady and Sasha you can meet the rest of the girls." All three of them stood to shake hands.

"What's your name?" Reign asked his little beauty. She smiled and tucked her hair behind her ear.

"Giselle," she responded. Reign felt himself getting lost in the depths of her eyes again.

"Okay Giselle, see you later tonight," he smiled almost too eagerly. Giselle grabbed onto Sasha's arms when she felt that she was going to stumble over her feet again. She smiled and nodded at Reign and backed out of the room with Sasha. When the door closed she turned to her best friend and punched her in the arm.

"What the hell was that for?!" Sasha cried out, holding her arm.

"That's for bringing me into that damn room knowing damn well I was not about to be dancing!" Sasha smirked.

"But you should be thanking me for getting you a job," Sasha scoffed.

"I don't have the job yet."

"We all know your skills is on point."

"And you wouldn't guess what else," Giselle said.

"What? What happened?" Sasha asked.

"The owner; Reign? He's my sexy mystery man," Giselle admitted. Sasha gasped.

"Oh shit! No wonder why the man kept looking at your fine ass!"

"Sasha shut up he was not looking at me," Giselle lied. She smiled when her friend turned and began walking back to the main room.

"You can sure choose em Giselle, he is sexy as hell. And he's a man in charge. You should have done some flirting or something. But don't worry, you'll be working with him enough to possibly get you some nookie." Giselle scoffed.

"Yeah right! I may daydream about a nookie but I sure as hell ain't gonna get none."

"Quit being shy," Sasha ordered. That was easy for Sasha to say but already even though Giselle felt some sort of attraction to him, she was very intimidated by him.

When they entered the main room, Sasha's hot

security guard looked straight at her. Sasha was teasing her friend about Reign, but now she was understanding what it felt like to be under the stare of a man so sexy that made you feel as if you were swimming in the deep sea with no oxygen left in your lungs.

"Maybe you oughta retire your vibrating dildo and sit on that," Giselle said. Sasha slapped her friend on the arm.

"And what? End up like you and Dean? No thanks. I need to see his dick up front before I make any commitments," Sasha smiled.

"You're such a bitch," Giselle laughed. Just as they went pass the security guard, Sasha smiled at him.

"See you tonight," she winked at him. His raised his brows and winked back at her but said nothing else. In that subtle wink, Sasha's heart was beating more quickly, and her cheeks were hot. Looks like Sasha should take some of her own advice. She never filled her life with so much activity to hide her loneliness, she admitted that she was a loner and accepted that. She however didn't allow many people to break through her barriers, and maybe she should start doing that. You never know who you could get close with once you strip yourself of your inhibitions and just let go.

Khloe paced back and forth in Reign's office. He was finishing up the paperwork on that Sasha girl. He'd requested that no other women be sent up to him. True, Khloe had chosen those other girls because she knew Reign would never hire them. They lacked fitness and seduction. But in the case that Reign did hire them, they wouldn't be a threat to her and Reign's relationship. Khloe done completely forgot about Sasha and her little friend and now they both were about to be working under Reign. The little one Khloe wasn't intimidated by. But Sasha, oh Khloe had to watch out for that bitch and make sure she didn't lay one finger on her man.

"Hungry?" Reign asked her, closing his binder. He either didn't see or didn't care about Khloe's obvious attitude.

"You realize I'm mad at you right?" she asked.

"For what?" he asked.

"The way you threatened me!" She said, even though she was angrier at the fact that he'd hired those two women.

"I told your ass to be quiet. You're so damn hard headed." Khloe just crossed her arms and looked at him.

"Come on, let me take you to eat something. Then I gotta fuck some manners into you." Khloe scoffed.

"Please, you can't fuck nothing into me," she said. Reign just smiled at her.

"In due time K, in due time. Come on." He grabbed his things and walked with her out of the club. They used the back entrance of the club and left, but when they turned on the street to walk down the strip to find a place for lunch, Khloe saw Sasha and Giselle standing in front of the club talking. Khloe immediately wrapped her arms around Reign as they walked past the two women. Sasha and Giselle made eye contact with Khloe as she walked hand in hand with Reign. Giselle was well aware that Khloe was showing off. She couldn't fault the woman because Reign was sexy as fuck, but Giselle was jealous of course.

"Don't worry bout that bitch," Sasha said. "Let's get a mimosa." Khloe could only smile when Sasha rolled her eyes and led her friend away. She wanted to make sure Sasha understood that Reign belonged to Khloe and that was not going to change.

# Chapter Seven

When all the females left from their interviews, Dalen secured the premises and locked all the doors until the club would reopen later that night. While the other guards went home, or went someplace else until later, Dalen climbed the back stairs of the club all the way to the top floor. He used a key and opened the single door that was located at the end of the hall. He entered a studio apartment that was his. He kicked off his boots and walked into the room, going to his small kitchen to pour himself a drink. Though it was just a studio apartment, Reign had furnished this place like it was a ten room mansion. All the furniture and fixings were brand new. It was a bachelor pad, except for the fact that Dalen was no bachelor. He was a simple broke man who was always struggling and fighting to stay above water. But he went without work for months and he couldn't afford his rent anymore. He was out on the streets until Reign came along.

He and Reign were childhood friends. Probably the only friends the each of them had. Dalen's parents were broke junkies, and Reign's mother was a stripper. They weren't winning any popularity contests. But Dalen always remembered Reign would steal money from his mother just to give to him, but Dalen's parents never used it for food or clothes. They just used it for a high. When Reign inherited the strip club, he hired Dalen immediately. But Dalen didn't tell his friend he was living at a shelter because he didn't have enough money. Reign found out where Dalen went after work and immediately did something about it. Dalen had too much pride to accept anything his friend was offering, but they came to an agreement. He would rent out this space for Dalen for a small sum until Dalen had enough money to buy his own place. It seemed fair enough and Dalen didn't mind not having to commute to get home.

Sitting on his bed, Dalen sipped his henny and coke. He rested back against the headboard and closed his eyes, taking in the silence of the place. Through his window he could only hear the birds of Miami. Behind his closed eyes, the image of that beautiful woman popped up. She was more than just beautiful, in fact Dalen couldn't find the right words to describe her. It was hard to even think about pursuing a woman when you barely had money to buy yourself clothes. Dalen had learned that his parents were not only high but they used his name to use credit for things they couldn't afford. Dalen learned the hard way that if he ever wanted his own place or hell, his own damn car his credit was too destroyed to make it happen. So not only was he struggling to just live, he was struggling to pay off all the shit he was left to clean up to secure his own damn bag. What woman would deal with a broke man with all that damn baggage?

A firm knock sounded at his door. There was only one person that knew he stayed up here, so he wasn't concerned about who it was.

"Come in," he said firmly. Reign opened the door and entered the room. He closed it behind him.

"What we drinking?" Reign smiled at his friend.

"Henny and coke," Dalen answered.

"That kinda day is it?" Reign kicked off his shoes and went to the kitchen. He searched the fridge and came out with a beer.

"You might not have a beer gut now but keep drinking that shit and that's exactly what you gonna get." Dalen teased. Reign rolled his eyes and flexed his muscles. He popped the cap on the beer and walked to Dalen's bed, dropping down and sighing hard.

"That kinda day is it?" Dalen repeated the words to his best friend.

"Khloe man, she's a fucking trip," he said.

"What'd she do?"

"I mean, nothing really. I just...sometimes she just annoying," Reign shrugged.

"That don't stop you from fucking her," Dalen answered truthfully.

"Of course it don't. Sex with that woman is more than satisfactory. But it's like she swears she owns me or some shit."

"I don't really get ya'll two. Like you want the woman to have your kids, but you haven't wifed her up? She acting like that cause she's trying to get you to see she wanna have that ring on that finger."

"I haven't wifed her up because we are still in an open relationship. None of us are ready for that commitment."

"No it's not that you're not ready it's the fact that you just don't want her to ultimately be your wife," Dalen told him. Reign looked at his friend.

"So what the fuck, you were watching Oprah or some shit today?" Reign asked. Dalen laughed.

"Nah, not at all. Just tryna make you see what's up. Be honest with yourself Reign you know it's true." Reign didn't say anything for a minute.

"Okay fine, so what if I'm not completely sure about marrying her? I just need to face the fact that she is all I have. At some point I'm gonna get tired of being lonely, and I know that I can turn to her and she'll be there. You know, you're one to talk. You're about the loneliest muthafucker I know." Dalen laughed again.

"What you want me to do? Invite women up to the studio apartment where my best friend is letting me sleep at on top of his club? I don't think so."

"I already told your dumbass I would rent you a house," Reign said.

"I'm a man Reign, not a little bitch. I'll earn my money and buy myself a house," Dalen told him. Reign shrugged.

"Fine then, you can do that and I respect it. I'm just surprised you ain't got blue balls." Both men laughed out loud.

"Just cause I don't bring women here don't mean I don't fuck." Reign's phone went off in his pocket. He took it out and placed it on the bed when he saw it was Khloe calling.

"You not gonna answer?" Dalen asked.

"I just fucked her from here to Timbuctoo, what the hell she got to call me for?" Reign questioned.

"Women are needy Reign. Understand that and you won't be so dumbfounded about what they do." Reign cut his eyes at his friend and picked up the phone.

"Yes Khloe?" Reign asked.

"Where did you go?" She asked.

"Why does it matter?" He prompted.

"I don't know, I'm just asking," she replied.

"I'll see you later Khloe, don't worry."

"I'm not worried. Do you want the kitchen to have dinner for you ready tonight?" She asked.

"Um yeah sure if you wanna do that," he sighed.

"Okay baby, see you later."

"Bye K." Reign hung up the phone and looked at Dalen who was smiling at him.

"You still don't want to wife her?" Dalen teased. "She's calling you to ask if you're alright." Reign scoffed.

"Yeah she's being nice now. She's just on an orgasm high right now." Reign stood and dug into his pockets. "Here I was meaning to give you this." Dalen looked at the folded envelope.

"What is it?" He asked.

"Just take it." Dalen took the envelope. When he unfolded it and looked inside he found 1,000 dollars.

"What the hell is this for?" Dalen asked. "And you know damn well I don't do that charity shit."

"Calm the fuck down. It's your check. I know you don't like going to the check cashing place so I'm just gonna give it to you in cash from now on. Cool with you?" Dalen nodded.

"Yeah cool, thanks man." Dalen sighed and took another sip of his drink. If it wasn't for this man, Dalen didn't know where he would be at the moment.

"Don't let pride keep you from asking me for what you need Dalen. I'm not gonna be living this luxurious life with my brotha out here struggling. What kind of man would that make me? And it's not like we just met either Dalen. We've been feeding each other since we were kids. Shouldn't be no difference now."

"Yeah it shouldn't but there is. When we were kids we weren't able to fend for ourselves, so we relied on each other. Now we're both grown. Shouldn't be no reason I should still be asking you for handouts Reign."

"Do you know why I hired you as my security guard?" Reign asked crossing his arms. "When we were little I couldn't defend myself. Everyone was out to kick my ass until you defended me. Even now if I'm bout to fuck someone up and you're at my back I feel confident as hell. If I told you someone tried to shoot me what would you do?"

"I'd kill them for you, you know that!" Dalen exclaimed.

"You think I'm too prideful to tell you I got my ass kicked and I need you to help me?" Dalen didn't answer. "Hell if a nigga comes at me that's 200 pounds heavier than me, you think I won't ask you to fuck him up for me since I know I'll get my ass kicked? When you're as close to someone as much as we are then all that judgement and pride goes out the window. I ain't scared to ask my family for help. So get that through your brain I'm always gonna make sure I do what I can to help even if you ask for it or not." When Dalen didn't answer, Reign just shrugged.

"See you tonight," Reign said walking towards the door. When he left, Dalen let out the breath he was holding. Even though he would try to keep denying it, deep inside he knew Reign was right. That was his family, and he would do anything for Reign. And he shouldn't expect Reign not to feel the same.

********

Giselle grunted hard as her head hit the headboard one last time before Dean toppled over her exhausted. She rolled her eyes and pushed him off her.

"You're like 500 pounds get off," she exaggerated.

"Oh, sorry baby," he smiled rolling off her. He reached for her to cuddle with him but she drew away.

"What's the matter?" He asked.

"I can't lay here, I got a gig tonight," she said. After drinks with Sasha after their meeting, Giselle was going to go home to prepare her makeup products, but Dean had practically begged her for sex so she caved in. She drove over to his home where he wined and dined her, then busted his traditional five minute nut. It was only after seven, and the both of them were scheduled to be at the club at 9pm. And she really didn't want to have to lay here with him and pretend that she was satisfied.

"Oh yeah? Where at?" He asked her.

"Pearls," she answered. Dean looked wide eyed at her.

"You 'bout to start stripping and you ain't talk to me about this shit first?!" He exclaimed.

"Calm down. I'm doing the makeup there. And

so what if I was stripping, what I got to tell you for?"

"Because I'm your man, you should tell me these things."

"Dean what we have is an open relationship," Giselle said. "That means I don't have to tell you shit, okay?" He sighed.

"Aight fine, just be careful and call me later." Giselle just raised her brows at him and went to get dressed. She did that in under five minutes and ran out that damn house. She stopped at home for her makeup and a nice shower before going over to Sasha's place.

"I can't find shit to wear!" Sasha exclaimed as she fumbled through her closet.

"I told you ass to get your outfit together hours ago!" Giselle said.

"And I been searching since! I don't even got lingerie. Ain't like I got a man to be sexy for." Giselle gave her friend a look. She tied her curls into a pony tail.

"Give me anything. Anything you not gonna wear again or you don't care for." Sasha searched her drawers and came up with a matching black and white skirt and top cheerleading uniform.

"I ain't gonna wear that again," Sasha said.

"You shouldn't," Giselle said. "It's so high school."

"What you gonna do with it?" Sasha asked.

"Not to worry. We got an hour. Get showered and pack a change of clothes and a shower pack for after your shift." Sasha nodded and went off to get things done. Giselle went to Sasha's small living room. In the corner of the room, Sasha had a sewing machine that belonged to her grandmother. Not wanting to throw out anything she had of the woman Sasha kept it, but she couldn't sew. While Giselle studied cosmetology and styling she learned how to sew. She used Sasha's machine more than she did.

Picking up a pair of scissors, she began cutting and sewing her friend a new outfit. She cut the black skirt until it was only a couple of inches long. She hemmed it out so it didn't look tacky. Ripping the shirt apart she made it into tight cropped halter top instead of just a regular bikini top. She made sure no strings were hanging down from where she cut. By the time she finished a half hour had passed. Going back into the bedroom, Sasha was out of the shower and packing a small bag.

"Here try this on," Giselle said. Sasha looked surprised at the outfit.

"You're so talented sometimes I just be feeling like a hater, but I can't even hate that much." Giselle laughed.

"Go on, put it on." Everything fit perfect as she put it on, but the skirt was so short, you could see every damn thing going on.

"What about my vag?" Sasha asked. "I'm dancing not riding dick," she said dryly.

"Simple. I know you have black spanks, or you can just wear your lace panties. In fact, I know you got white lace panties to match." Sasha thought for a moment then went back to her drawers and pulled out the perfect panties.

"See, now you look hot. Come on let's get outta here." Sasha took off the outfit and packed it in her bag. She threw on a pair of sweat shorts and a tank top.

Giselle was wearing a pair of shorts herself with another halter top but this one covered her stomach, so she tucked the bottom into her high waist shorts. And just because she knew she was about to be around a whole lot of tall slender women, she wore wedge heels to give herself some height. Giselle knew that she was going to be overshadowed anyway; it didn't matter if she wore heels or not. She was just that unnoticeable.

When they arrived at the club yet again, Sasha felt a little bit nervous but not as much. She was dancing tonight, and dancing was her thing, right? By the reaction she got last night, she thought dancing was the easy part. Fitting in with the other girls may be different however. If they were all like Khloe, then she and Giselle had a problem. She really didn't want to fight in Reign's club, but if a bitch got too mouthy she couldn't promise not to shut them up with her fists.

"Ay, yo!" Someone shouted when they entered the club. Both girls looked around. The security guard from earlier approached them. Again, Sasha's hormones jumped at seeing him. His black t-shirt stretched taut across his big broad chest.

"New girls," he greeted. "Reign wanted me to give you orders." Sasha crossed her arms and pouted at him even though she was thinking about kissing his lips.

"That's not our names," Sasha said. "Ay yo, and new girls ain't our names." He nodded.

"Right. My bad. That was rude of me."

"Damn right it was." Giselle looked at Sasha wondering why she was pestering the man. Sasha clearly thought he was sexy, why was she tryna run him away? Instead of getting offended, the guard just smiled at her and pressed his finger into the dimple on Sasha's chin. She jumped in surprise but let him touch her.

"What's your name, dimple?" He asked her. Sasha tried to be offended but she just couldn't. He was just terrible sexy.

"Sasha," she mumbled. He smiled at her and then looked at Giselle and nodded.

"Reign would like you to do your audition in front of the crowd tonight. Around 1am, you'll get on stage and do ya thing. He'll determine from there if he likes it or not, which I don't doubt that he will." Sasha caught the last bit of words clearly and understood just what he meant.

"What's your name little miss?" He asked Giselle. She was unfazed by his words whereas Sasha could barely stop looking at the man.

"Giselle," she replied.

"Boss says he wants to see some of your work. He's trusting you to work on the girls tonight."

"Okay," Giselle squeaked. Sasha kept her eye on the guard as she began to walk slowly away with Giselle next to her. Not once did he look away. Stopping in her tracks, she faced him.

"So, what do they call you?" She asked him.

"They call me the muscle," he said. Sasha thought he was serious until she saw a small smirk curve his tender lips. She couldn't help smiling herself.

"Clown," Sasha smiled. He winked at her.

"You can call me whatever you like, Dimple," he said.

"Let's start with the name your mama gave ya," she said.

"Dalen," he answered. Sasha felt as if he said his name with added seduction. He had to have said it that way because goosebumps erupted against her skin and her body wouldn't just react over a name, would it?

"Thanks for giving us the message, Dalen," Sasha said finally. Before he could reply to her, a shout from the club entrance caught his attention. His smile dropped in a second as he turned back to his job. Sasha watched as his presence dominated over the little argument the females were having. He separated them and said something firmly. Sasha couldn't hear what he said but both the females nodded in obedience and went their separate ways. When he looked back at Sasha he gave her a slight smile but went in through a door next to the exit. Giselle carefully pulled onto Sasha's arm.

"Come on now, he's got work to do. Let's go get dressed." Sasha reluctantly turned from him and followed Giselle.

"I've never seen you that attracted to a man," Giselle said to her. Sasha shrugged.

"Yeah, me either. But he works here. He's no

doubt getting pussy every night."

"Right, so a little pussy from you won't be a big deal," Giselle joked. "Give him some and just get it over with." Sasha pushed her friend playfully.

"You're such a bitch," she smiled. She knew just what her best friend meant, and thinking about it, Sasha didn't see it as such a bad idea. Dalen was fine as hell, and well, Sasha was getting tired of her toys. She wanted something real to hold onto. And Dalen was more than real.

Going through the back hall, they found the entrance to the dressing room. Giselle opened the door to the room. It was large and luxurious, each girl having her own space and cubicle to do their makeup and get changed. When the two women walked in, all conversation stopped. Every woman in the room turned and looked at Giselle and Sasha.

"Um, hi," Sasha said. "I'm-"

"You're the new girl," someone said. "Khloe told us all about you."

"Yeah. I still have my audition later."

"Good luck with that." Sasha and Giselle

exchanged looks. "Oh, and you're the so called makeup artist. We heard about you too."

"So, who are you?" Giselle asked. The tall woman stood and put her hands on her hips.

"Ginger. But I'll let you know that I don't need any of your little makeup tips. So I don't need you." Giselle gave the woman a look. But then just like her, the other women agreed with her. Sasha just patted Giselle on the back.

"Is there anywhere for me to get changed?" Sasha asked. This time all the girls laughed.

"In the corner," Ginger said, pointing to the far corner of the room away from the rest of the women. But there was no, cubicle, vanity, or even a mirror. Just a plain ole corner. It was clear these women didn't like anyone new coming into their space.

"Great! I'll just go get ready then." Sasha pulled Giselle to the corner as she dragged her suitcase and makeup equipment behind her.

"So what the fuck is their problem?" Giselle asked. "It's not like we forced our way in here, Reign hired us!"

"Look, don't trip. Just worry about what we came here to do for ourselves," Sasha advised.

"But I can't do what I need if none of these bitches want me to do their makeup!"

"Relax. Do my makeup and help me get dressed. Don't worry about them." Even though Sasha was giving encouraging words, she wasn't that inspired her damn self. Reign cared about the women that worked here. If they all came together and requested Giselle and Sasha to be put out, he'd do it.

"If you say so," Giselle said. She took a vacant stool and sat Sasha down. From there, she made up Sasha and helped her fix up her hair. As the night went on before the club opened, the other women in the dressing room didn't say anything to Giselle or Sasha, but they could hear them snickering and making comments about what Giselle and Sasha was doing. Giselle tried to ignore them but it was hard not to tell them to shut the hell up. As fighting was sure to get both of them kicked out, Giselle just kept calm.

"Okay girls, time to line up," Khloe called, entering the dressing room. Giselle finished the touches on Sasha's outfit, snipping away at any loose threads.

"Kill these bitches," Giselle told her friend. Sasha smiled and jumped up. Khloe immediately skinned up her face at them.

"Um, not you two," Khloe said. "The lineup is for the real working girls. Reign will talk to ya'll later." This time it was Sasha who was feeling the urge to slap someone. Why was everyone giving them the cold shoulder?

"Okay I guess," Sasha mumbled. She plopped back down on her stool and watched as all the other girls lined up and walked out of the dressing room laughing to each other.

"No one said this was easy," Giselle said, leaning against the wall next to Sasha.

Reign watched as all his girls lined up in the main room like they did every night. He looked them all over, walking up and down the line. Khloe stood in her perfection like she always did, so he never had a comment for her. But he noticed that the makeup and clothing options for the rest of the girls did not look as good as Khloe.

"Girls," Reign sighed. "It's not looking good. I keep tellin' ya'll to stop looking so cheap." Their makeup looked as if they worked on the street corner than in an actual high end club. Reign's mind flashed to Giselle. That's when he realized she and the other new girl weren't here.

"Dalen," Reign turned to talk to his security guard.

"What's up?"

"The two new girls showed?" He asked.

"Yeah I gave them the orders you told me." Reign nodded and looked back at the line of girls in the room. If Giselle was here, and his orders were to make up his girls, and now they were here looking a hot mess, he was having doubts about how talented the cute little woman was.

"Where are the newbies?" Reign asked the girls. It was Khloe that spoke up first.

"I told them we were lining up but I guess they never followed us out," she shrugged. Reign nodded. He went back over to where Dalen stood in front of the floor office. Reign entered the room to use the intercom to speak into the dressing room.

"Ladies," he said. When they didn't answer he figured they didn't know where or how to use the intercom system. "It's Reign. Get out to the main room. Now." By the time he walked out of the office, he could hear them arguing with each other quietly. When they entered the main room, they elbowed each other but then they straightened and walked silently. Reign looked at Giselle and when their eyes locked he felt as if he'd gotten punched in the gut. He honestly couldn't believe how beautiful she was.

"We work on a schedule here," Reign said. "I fine for tardiness because I simply hate it." Sasha's mouth opened to say something but Giselle elbowed her. "When I call for a line up, that means every girls needs to be out here. Understood?" Both girls just looked at him. "I asked you a question," he said softly.

"Yes Reign," Sasha said. He looked at Giselle.

"Yes," She practically whispered. He motioned to the line.

"If you please Sasha, join the line." Sasha

hurried into the line. Reign noticed then that she was wearing a silk robe. She'd probably rushed out of the dressing room forgetting to take it off. But he would talk to her in a minute. He turned back and looked at his little beauty.

"Giselle, I asked you to make up the girls. Is that the order Dalen gave you?" She just nodded. "I understand that you're looking for a place here and I had high hopes, but you didn't really give me much to go on here. I'm not that impressed." Giselle's brows furrowed.

"I wouldn't be impressed either," she said quietly.

"If you ain't impressed by your own work, how can I hire you?" He asked. Her mouth opened and she backed up a step and looked at him up and down."

"I didn't do their makeup. In fact, I would never do makeup as tacky as that." Reign was shocked at her attitude. She seemed so shy but just then she showed him that she wasn't afraid to speak her mind.

"Why didn't you?" he asked.

"Your girls told me they were too good and

didn't need my help so I let it be." Reign turned and looked at the girls. All of them were avoiding eye contact, so he already knew what Giselle said was true. His eyes landed on Sasha.

"Ae you planning to dance in your robe?" He teased her.

"Oh, uh no," she laughed. She undid the robe and let it fall to the ground. He honestly wasn't expecting much, but when he saw her outfit he was indeed shocked. The short skirt and white lace panties paired together perfectly with the halter top. Reign walked over to her and looked at her more closely. That's when he saw her face was made up beautifully. Her makeup matched her outfit and she wore a bright red lipstick. The highlights and contours of her face gave her beauty so much depth. Reign took her hand and led her in front of all the girls.

"This ladies, is what you should look like," Reign said. "This is what I'm looking for when I line you up."

"What does this chick know about anything?" Khloe said. "Far as I can tell she's the one that looks cheap." Reign didn't answer her. He shot her a look and she quieted.

"She's right," Sasha said. "I don't know about anything. This is all Giselle." Reign looked at his little beauty, standing quietly. "She did everything from my hair, to my makeup, and my outfit."

"Your outfit?" Reign asked.

"Yes, she made my outfit. Like literally made it. Once upon a time this was my cheerleading uniform." Reign was shocked at Giselle's talent, and he strangely found himself even more attracted to her.

"Really?" Reign asked, looking at Giselle. She only nodded. "Well I am appreciative of your work it looks very good Giselle." Reign turned back to his girls.

"This is what I want ya'll to look like," Reign said. "So since you all think you're hot shit, how about this. No one will be allowed to dance until they have had their outfit and makeup approved by Giselle." Giselle's mouth fell open. She was not expecting him to give her so much power. Everyone else wasn't expecting that either and they were not happy about it. Khloe could feel her face getting hot. She didn't like the way Reign was standing Sasha in front of everyone like she was some queen. Khloe especially didn't like how Reign was looking at her. He used to look at Khloe that way. She was the perfection he loved, and now this bitch was here and it was really making Khloe angry.

"I don't like this at all Reign!" Khloe snapped. "You can't just change up the rules to fit new people in. They have to fit themselves to our rules, and our rules says we can wear what we want. So what if she can do makeup that don't got nothing to do with us. I never come out here looking cheap, you love the way I look. So now I have to get approval for how I look? And this bitch here tore up a cheerleading uniform and you think she doesn't look cheap? Why you giving them special treatment?"

"You need to watch your mouth Khloe. And I mean it." He answered. Khloe heard the serious edge to his voice but she just couldn't let it go. She crossed her arms and tapped her foot in anger.

"Does anyone have a problem with getting approval from Giselle first?" Reign asked the group. All of them began to express their unhappiness. "Okay, so if you have a problem with my rules, there's the door," Reign said. That shut everyone up. They looked at the door but no one moved.

"That's what the fuck I thought," Reign said.

"How would you feel if I left?" Khloe asked. Reign shrugged and motioned to the door.

"Go ahead and leave then Khloe." Her mouth fell open.

"It's that easy that you'll let me walk away?" She asked.

"Yes, it's that easy Khloe, because you're going to make me lose my cool. I put up with your shit but you're crossing that line and you know it too."

"You only put up with my shit because I suck your dick," she stated. She knew she said the wrong thing when his eyes went wide for a second.

"Are you out ya fucking mind?" He snapped. "In fact, I got a better lesson for your ass."

Giselle felt like she should be frightened, or concerned for how this man was going to handle the situation. The way he raised his voice should be a call for uncertainty within her attraction to him. But looking at his face, and listening to his deep voice demand respect made her panties wet. Her eyes were glued to his strong body waiting for him to do what he was going to do, her attraction increasing by the minute. She just loved it when a man was forceful. Even though Dean was a disappointment, she had a gut feeling that Reign was not the same. If he said he was going to fuck you, then he was going to fuck you.

"Since you think that I put up with your shit just for a simple dick sucking."

"Well you do don't you!" Khloe said. Reign cut his eyes at her.

"Anyone think they can suck my dick better than she can?" Reign asked the girls. Giselle scoffed under her breath and went to put her hand up, but Sasha forced her hand down and gave Giselle a look. She was right, Giselle wasn't here to suck his dick, she was just here to work and maybe she couldn't even handle him anyway. All of the other girls however raised their hands.

"You fucking bitches!" Khloe snapped.

"So many women to choose from," Reign said

looking at all of the women. "Ginger," he called out. She stepped forward and licked her lips. "You look like you're up to the job," he said.

"You know I am baby," she said.

"Go up to my office and wait for me."

"Are you seriously gonna let her suck your dick Reign?" Khloe asked.

"So that way you understand that I don't need you to be around to get my dick sucked. I put up with your shit simply because I want to. You should know better than any of these girls not to push my buttons Khloe, and you should know better what your role in my life is supposed to be. I don't give a fuck how mad you are, you say some bullshit out ya mouth like that again I'm gonna let you watch me fuck each and every female in this place. Go to my fucking office right now," he ordered. Giselle's panties were almost soaked all the way through. God damn this man was sexy as fuck!

"What for?" Khloe asked quietly. "You already want Ginger to suck you off," she pouted.

"Yeah I do, but what kind of lesson would I be

teaching you if I didn't let you watch her do it?" Giselle stared in awe at him. What the fuck was wrong with her? She shouldn't be mesmerized by what he was doing. Actually it was kind of fucked up. But for some reason, he was talking like a straight boss and she loved it. Khloe walked away quietly as Ginger followed her to his office.

"You all have the schedule, nothing has changed," Reign sighed looking back at the girls. "Sasha, you're on at 1 A.M. You'll dance alone for 20 minutes then two girls will join you."

"Yes Reign," she said.

"Since Khloe just pissed me off with her bullshit, I don't want none of ya'll on that stage until you're all cleaned up. Giselle fix them up. If you refuse to have her do your makeup then just leave." Everyone just nodded. When Reign turned to leave he looked directly at Giselle. Her cheeks felt hot looking at him. She could only imagine him fucking the life outta her and dominating her. She licked her lips, and tried to look away but it was no use. She didn't think she was ever entranced by a man like this before. She could probably guess this is exactly what Sasha felt when she couldn't take her eyes off Dalen.

"Showtime is 12am Giselle. Can you handle that?" He asked her softly.

"I can handle a lot," she answered. She didn't mean to sound so sexual, it literally slipped her tongue. His surprised gasp turned all her lust and arousal into embarrassment. She looked away from him and all but ran away as she went back to the dressing room.

"Come on girls!" She called. "A lot to do, little time!"

Reign watched Giselle's plump bottom as she walked off. He honestly couldn't take his eyes off her and he didn't give a damn who saw him staring. All the girls followed her but Reign didn't stop looking. It wasn't until he felt a slap in the arm that he turned his attention from Giselle. Sasha was looking at him inquisitively. He cursed under his breath when she gave him a knowing look.

"Whatcha looking at?" She asked in a sing song voice. Reign tried not to smile at her.

"I don't know what you talking about," he said.

She batted her lashes.

"To me, well to me it looked like you were looking at Giselle's ass." Yup, he was caught.

"So what Sash?" he asked. She shrugged.

"Well, I'm a woman and I can't help but look at her ass, so I don't blame you. That girl definitely got it going on." Reign's façade finally broke and he smiled.

"Okay ya caught me. Her ass...it's a nice one I admit."

"Do you wanna touch it? Spank it? Caress it?" she inquired. For a second Reign saw Giselle's ass in his mind again. He bit his bottom lip as he could imagine getting his hands on that ass of hers. Because her ass was fake, when he had sex with Khloe from the back, her ass did nothing. It was big, but it just did nothing. But Giselle? Reign shook his head. She was all real, and he could bet his left nut her ass would jiggle, bounce, and clap if he pounded her from the back. Shit, he was getting hard.

"I think I got business to attend to in my office," Reign said. Sasha smiled knowingly.

"Alright go on I guess. I'll just go and talk with

Giselle about my future outfits." Reign pulled her arm then put a finger under her chin, forcing her to look up in his eyes.

"Don't you dare tell that woman I was looking at her ass," he said. Sasha laughed.

"You are my boss after all," she said. She smiled and walked off. Reign shook his head and headed to his office to take care of his business.

"I don't care what he says he's gonna do to you, you better not put his dick in your mouth!" He heard Khloe snap when he entered the office. Both of the women looked up at him. Since he was still hard from thinking about Giselle, he was ready for a release.

"Reign, don't-"

"I don't wanna hear it," he said, cutting Khloe off. "Ginger come here," he ordered, undoing his jeans. When he pulled his dick out, Ginger was like a child who'd been giving candy. She dropped to her knees in front of him, grabbing the base of his dick. She shoved it into her mouth as if she'd been waiting for the chance to suck him off. Reign was shocked at her urgency, as she basically gobbled him down.

Khloe watched in shock as Ginger didn't hold anything back while sucking off Reign. She was literally going at it like she was sucking a damn lollipop. Her head bobbed back and forth smoothly. Khloe couldn't do anything as she watched her man be pleasured by another woman. He was biting his lip as Ginger deep throated him. He tried to pull his dick from her mouth as his release neared, but she pressed his body against her, keeping his dick deep in her mouth. Khloe saw the telltale sign on Reigns' release. He snapped his eyes shut and grunted, holding Ginger's head still as he came into her mouth. Like the savage she was, Ginger sucked it all up, not releasing his dick until it was soft in her mouth. She stood and licked her lips, smiling as she looked at Khloe.

"Damn Khloe," she said. "If I were you'd I'd never upset this man. But don't worry, if you do upset him, I'll be here to take care of him." Khloe lunged for Ginger. Reign quickly stepped in between them and grabbed Khloe around the waist.

"Get out Ginger," he ordered. Ginger ran out of the room. Reign closed and locked the door before he put Khloe down.

"I hope you're satisfied!" She yelled at him, slapping him on the chest.

"I hope you learned your lesson," he answered. "I would never put up with you because you can just suck my dick. You straight up disrespected me in front of everyone, so I hope you feel just what the hell I felt."

"Whatever Reign." She rolled her eyes then sidestepped him and went to leave the office.

"Do not go and attack her Khloe. My fighting rules extend to you as well." She just huffed.

"I need to get ready for my dance," she stated. "I don't got time to worry about you or that bitch."

In that moment Reign thought maybe he went too far. Maybe he shouldn't have done that in front of Khloe but it was already done. And with the way she was running her mouth, she deserved it. He knew that she was going to retaliate in some way, but he just didn't know how. Either way it was all said and done and there was nothing he could do to change it.

When Giselle finished all the makeup for the

girls, she was alone in the dressing room. She packed her things away to set it up for when she was ready to leave. Looking at her phone, she had texts from Dean, but she wasn't interested in answering any of them so she just shut her phone off and put it away. She told him she was working, so he didn't have to be blowing up her phone in the first place. She thought about leaving, but she figured she'd stay and enjoy a drink while she watched Sasha take over the stage. She left the dressing room and went towards the main room. She could already hear the shouts and the cheers of the crowd at whoever was dancing. When she saw it was Ginger, she rolled her eyes and went over to the bar plopping down on a stool.

"Malibu Bay Breeze," she ordered over the noise. The bartender nodded and fixed her drink. Just as she began sipping her drink, the security guard came over and joined her.

"Hey what's up," he greeted. She smiled.

"Hi."

"Intense first night isn't it?" he asked. Giselle nodded.

"Yeah, your boss. Well, he's something else. And these girls. They're all bitches." Dalen laughed at her.

"You'll get used to them. Reign, he's a pretty cool guy actually. Khloe just came out of her mouth wrong and well, she paid for it."

"True, she fucked up," Giselle shrugged. Dalen looked at her for a moment without saying anything. She was a very pretty woman, with a quiet seduction about her.

"Can't wait for you friend to go on," Dalen said. "No doubt she'll kill it." Giselle looked at him and smirked.

"You like her don't you?" She asked. Dalen scoffed.

"I don't even know her," he answered.

"Alright, so you want to fuck her don't you?" Dalen went to deny it, but then he closed his mouth. Yeah, he couldn't really deny that fact.

"Maybe I do," he admitted. "But don't tell her that."

"I don't need to tell her," Giselle said. "You'll tell her yourself." Dalen was a man of confidence, but

Sasha was truly a woman of worth and he couldn't just bring her up to his small studio. She deserved more than that.

"I'll admire from afar," he said.

"We'll see how long that lasts," Giselle teased. Dalen thought she was only playing around with him, but when the room quieted, and Sasha walked out onto the stage, his heart leapt in his chest. His body was becoming aware of her presence and he couldn't stop looking at her. Blood pooled to his dick when he saw the sexy white panties under the small black skirt she was wearing. So maybe Giselle was right. He couldn't just watch Sasha from afar for too long. She was too desirable for that.

"I don't think she's up for what I wanna do with her," Dalen said. Giselle just sipped her drink and shrugged.

"You'll never know until you find out for yourself. Just know that she loves a man in charge."

"I'll keep that in mind."


At 1am, Reign left his office to go watch Sasha

dance. He knew she would be good and he'd had his mind set on hiring her anyway but he figured he'd see how the crowd reacted to her. Just as he got to the main room he saw Dalen and Giselle at the bar smiling and talking. A strange feeling came over him as he pictured himself going over to them and breaking them apart. He would never cock block his brother, but he definitely didn't want Dalen talking to that particular woman. That was his woman. Reign didn't know what gave him the right to think that she was his, but he just knew he never wanted a woman like he wanted her.

The moment Dalen walked away from Giselle, Reign hurried over to her. He slid in behind her. She nearly jumped out of her clothes when she felt him behind her.

"Sorry about that," he said "It's tight around here." She chuckled uneasily but didn't move away.

"You gotta warn a woman before you do that," she said.

"Sorry little bit," he replied. He looked towards the stage, watching as Sasha walked on. Giselle started cheering. When 'Pony', by Ginuwine started, Sasha grabbed onto the pole and did her thing. Her body moved expertly as she twirled on the pole. Even off the pole, her hips moved rhythmically. What Reign liked the most was that her personality screamed across the entire room. It almost forced people to cheer for her. Reign liked the connection she was making with everyone including the woman.

When her solo was up, she backed away to let the other girls that came on shine. She even blended and danced with them when Reign knew she thought they were bitches. It showed that she knew how to put her feelings aside and work. Even though she was letting the girls have their moment, the crowd kept gravitating towards her and sticking money in her outfit.

"She's amazing," Reign said.

"Tell me about it," Giselle responded. "By the way, where's your woman? I been dying to see her dance. She got a lot of mouth so I'm betting she should be the best dancer here." Reign was surprised by her words, but he knew that there was something else behind that innocent look she carried. She wasn't a woman afraid to speak her mind.

"Actually," Reign started. "She's good but I think Sasha tops her. Khloe can't really handle the crowds, she's more of a one on one type of girl."

"Figures," Giselle shook her head. The moment she took the last sip of her drink, Reign ordered her a new one. She gave him one of those smiles that made his knees weak.

"So, you like my work on the girls? Can I keep coming back?" Giselle asked.

"Of course little bit, I thought you figured that out already."

"Just making sure," she said.

"The girls didn't give Sasha a place to dress," Giselle said. "They put her in the corner. And if you want me to do their wardrobe I'll need some space myself."

"Not to worry I'll take care of you." Reign just wanted to pat her hand to reassure her, but when he touched her soft skin, he didn't let go. Soft electricity poured into him as he kept contact to where he as holding her. He took her hand fully into his and examined it.

"You have blisters," he said, seeing her fingertips were red.

"Yeah, I did some work on their wardrobe. I don't have a sewing machine, or anything so I was just using basic needle and thread. With one outfit I'm okay, but with over 5 girls needing some sort of alteration I put these hands to work." Reign massaged her fingers. Uncharacteristically for him, he placed her hand against his lips and kissed her fingers. When he looked at her, her eyes were low. She drew her bottom lip into her mouth and nibbled it.

"I'll make sure to set you up so you don't have to do that again," he assured her. Giselle was too lost in his stare to fully understand what he was saying. All she knew was that she didn't want him to ever stop touching her. But of course all good things must come to an end. He let her hand go and turned to flag down the bartender. He ordered a single patron shot that he gulped down.

"I got paperwork to finish," he said as his chest burned from the alcohol. Giselle nodded but she couldn't help her disappointment.

"Thanks for talking with me," Giselle said.

"See you tomorrow, but come in the afternoon."

"Why?" She asked

"We'll talk," he said. They looked at each other again, and when their eyes connected, they couldn't stop looking at each other. Giselle began to wonder what he was thinking. Could he tell that she was thinking about him sexually? That she was forcing herself not to kiss him? Giselle just knew that if she tried to kiss him, he would probably stop her and ask just what the hell she was doing. He probably thought she was small and cute but not sexy or fuckable like every man thought of her. That's why she was considering keeping Dean in her life.

"Have a...have a good night," Giselle stammered. He smiled at her and began to lean forward. Giselle's heart stopped beating for a second as anticipation coursed through her body. Was he about to kiss her? Giselle stared at his lips, as they got closer to her face. She didn't know just what to do or how to respond, but if he was going to kiss her, she needed to make sure she left him wanting more. She had to prove she wasn't just some little kid. She puckered her lips and closed her eyes. It seemed that eternity was passing as she waited to feel his sweet lips against hers. Just as she opened her eyes to see what was taking so long, she felt him press his lips against her forehead. Giselle gasped, and backed away from him, moving his hand from her head where he held it. He looked in shock himself at her reaction. Giselle couldn't help but feel like she was a teenager or something and he was kissing her goodnight like a kid sister. Who was she to think that this man who was no doubt in the dreams of all the women he worked around, would take her serious. That he would see her as what she felt like on the inside. Trying not to say something she would regret, she snatched her drink from the bar counter. She looked him up and down before sliding off her stool and walking away.

Reign just sat there thinking about what the hell he did wrong. He honestly was going to hold her and kiss those sweet lips of hers, but he thought it was too much. They barely knew each other and he didn't want to come off like a dog. He just couldn't help how bad his insides were burning to touch her, to kiss her, to hold her...to...to do everything to her. He thought kissing her on the forehead was a gesture to let her know he wanted her, but he wasn't going to be a dog about it. That surely backfired. She looked disgusted and disappointed at the same time, and Reign couldn't figure out why.

## Chapter Eight

"Tell me how you want it," Reign whispered in her ear. Giselle was racked with goosebumps when she felt his hard body press against hers from behind. Just before she and Sasha left the club, he grabbed onto her arm and led her away. Not knowing where he was taking her, she followed his lead like a puppy. She'd thought he was going to shun her for the way she just left him at the bar, but now he was back and he was on a mission. She couldn't decipher what made him so bold to be doing what he was doing now, but Giselle wasn't going to stop him. He dragged her to his office and shut them inside.

"You want me don't you?" He asked her, caressing her arms. Giselle just nodded as her body was clammy with arousal. She was on the verge of coming and all he was doing was touching her arms. His hard body against hers felt more pleasurable than any dick Dean had been giving her.

"You know I want you," she said. "You can see the way I look at you."

"That's why I'm gonna give you what you want," he said. "But I need to know how you want it Giselle." He brought his arms around her waist and unbuttoned her shorts. Slowly, he pushed them down over her hips bringing her panties down at the same time.

"I want it however you want to give it to me," she gasped. When she heard his zipper go down, arousal leaked out of her vagina, preparing herself for him.

"Lay your hands flat against my desk," he ordered. She did as he asked, bending over slightly. When she felt the tip of his fat cock brush against her opening she couldn't resist the moan that erupted from her throat.

"I've had dreams about being in your sweet

pussy," he whispered. "And now I'm going to make this pussy mine." She clenched her muscles as she felt his thick head breach her opening.

Giselle jumped awake at someone pounding at her door. She looked all around her to find that she wasn't in Reign's office about to receive hot steamy sex. She groaned and looked at the time. It was only 10am. She came home from the club at 4 in the morning. She felt moisture between her thighs recognizing the fact that she was truly having a wet dream about this man. How fucking crazy was that?

More banging broke the silence of her house. Who was really up this early knocking on her door? Cursing, she got out of bed and stumbled around. She was wearing a simple silk nightie that she pulled over herself and fell into bed. She was too tired to even think or do anything else but sleep.

As she walked to the door, the knocking continued. Looking through her peephole, she saw Dean standing there with his arms crossed. Groaning loudly, she opened the door and looked him straight in the face.

"What the fuck do you want?" She asked him. She of course couldn't help feeling angry that she was awoken from her precious dream. A dream that would have made her cum more than Dean ever did.

"Watch your fucking mouth Giselle. I been calling you all night, why you been ignoring me? I told you already that I hate to be ignored."

"I told you I was working. So why are you blowing my phone up in the first place?" He clenched his teeth and glared at her.

"I decided I don't want you working at that place anymore. I can provide for you," he stated.

"Hell no, I don't think so," Giselle said. "We are not in a relationship I told you that already. It's open until we are both ready for commitment. I don't need you taking care of me or giving me shit. Besides, I want to work there."

"Is there a reason you want to work there?" He asked.

"The money is great and I love what I do. How about that for a reason?" Money came as no problem for Dean since he owned a gym and kickboxing arena. That's where he and Giselle had met. But Giselle wasn't vain, and she didn't need a man's money to want to be with them.

"Are you working today?" He asked her. She nodded. "If you're gonna be gone all night and most of the day Giselle when are you going to have time for us?"

"I don't know Dean. Honestly I'm just tired right now I can't deal with this conversation. We can have it when I'm not falling over from drowsiness."

"You're just putting it off Giselle, don't think I can't see right through it," he accused.

"So what Dean? I literally don't have to talk to you if I don't want to. And I know you came here for a fucking but guess what? You ain't getting none."

"So you gonna be gone all last night, and then all night tonight and you mean to tell me you won't give me some fucking pussy?"

"Yeah that's what I mean. Besides I don't have the energy right now."

"You're something else," Dean snapped. "You

got one job! One damn job and that's to make sure I'm satisfied. You're doing a pretty fucked up job so far." Giselle couldn't believe what she was hearing. She was doing a fucked up job at satisfying him? There were so many words rotating in her mind to say to him, so she did the best thing she could do at the moment. Slammed the door in his face. She was ready to let him go with that insult and forget about it, but then he began pounding on her door.

"Open this fucking door Giselle!" He yelled. Fuck sparing his feelings. Giselle swung the door back open. Even though he was taller and bigger than she, she stepped up to him. Looking up at him, she poked his chest.

"How many times you made me come?" She snapped at him. "You think putting me in missionary is satisfying? What's my favorite position? You can criticize me about not pleasuring you but when we fuck you're the only one that gets the pleasure. My pussy makes you come all over yourself so much that you don't even give a fuck about if I reached an orgasm or not. So you should be the last person talking about I'm doing a fucked up job at pleasuring you. How bout you come the fuck back to my face when you learn how to give me a fucking orgasm. So right now you can fuck off!" She yelled. She slammed the door shut in his face again. She waited at the door for him to start knocking and yelling again, but nothing happened. She waited another 2 minutes until she heard his car start up and drive off. She punched her front door in her anger.

"Fuck!" She cried out, as she bruised her knuckles. She shook her hand out and looked at her hand. Her skin was split on her middle knuckle.

"Why me?" She asked, shaking her head and going back to her room. She honestly felt as if she couldn't get a break. First she was dreaming that she was about to get it on with a sexy ass man, only to have it interrupted by a man who couldn't touch her G-spot and he had the audacity to say she couldn't satisfy him. Wasn't that some straight bullshit? What a way to start off the morning.

********

Dalen unlocked the doors to the club the moment Reign drove into the parking lot. Dalen always opened the club for Reign by 11am. He was in charge of managing the cleaning crew when they came in. Since they knew he was going to be there, most of the dancers came back to practice routines by 2pm. When Reign entered the club, he clapped hands with Dalen in greeting. He gave Dalen his favorite iced coffee and tossed him a bag of donuts.

"Is Khloe here yet?" Reign asked. Dalen shook his head as he ate his donut.

"She been ignoring me," Reign said. "I been calling her."

"You didn't think she'd be happy about that stunt you pulled last night did you?" Dalen smiled. "It was boss shit, but you know Khloe holds a grudge hard."

"Yeah but it wasn't even that big a deal. It's not like I fucked Ginger," Reign shrugged.

"You wouldn't imagine how big a deal it is to a woman bro." Reign sucked his teeth.

"Page me when she gets here, okay? And um, the new girl, her too."

"Which new girl?" Dalen asked, already feeling

a jealous heat in his heart about Sasha being alone with Reign. Everyone female that came in this place was obsessed with Reign. He'd watched his friend turn down so many women but he'd also seen when he gave in to those women. The last thing Dalen wanted was his pretty dancer all over Reign.

"The little one," Reign answered. Dalen sighed in relief.

"Okay I'll tell her." Reign turned to walk away but then turned back to Dalen.

"What you think about her?" Reign asked.

"What I think about who?" Dalen quizzed.

"The little one idiot," Reign smiled.

"What you mean what I think about her?" Dalen was puzzled.

"What you think I mean?" Reign asked. Dalen chuckled.

"She's cute," he answered. "And very talented." When Dalen looked at his friend, he noticed that Reign was giving him a look. He didn't quite understand.

"The hell you looking at me like that for?" Dalen asked. "You the one that asked me what I thought of her."

"No reason," he said. "See ya later." Reign turned and walked away. He knew he shouldn't be, but he was a little upset Dalen thought his little beauty was cute. When Dalen thought a woman was cute, he went about pursuing them. Reign didn't think he could be around to watch his little beauty be courted by another man. Jealousy was not a trait that Reign ever carried. This time however, it felt like jealously would creep into his body at seeing that cute little woman with any man but him. Which was stupid because he was very much still involved with Khloe even though their relationship was not exclusive.

By 2pm, as some of the girls walked into the open doors, Dalen couldn't help but look for Sasha. He didn't expect her to show up because she didn't have to be here, but he was still hopeful. He still had a hard on from watching her dance last night. It was so strange to him because he'd never gotten hard from watching any of the other girls dance before. He felt like he was immune to their sex because he just didn't get aroused or felt the need to have sex with them. His last hookup was months ago and he didn't even notice how long he'd went without sex until he laid eyes on Sasha. It was like all his hormones were kicking into overdrive. His balls were so heavy it felt like they were dragging on the floor between his legs.

After almost all the women were present, Dalen gave up hope that Sasha was going to show up. She probably didn't even know the girls came here this early. And what the hell was Dalen so eager for? It's not like he was going to do anything when he saw her anyway.

"Hey Khloe," Dalen said as Khloe entered.

"What do you want?" She snapped.

"Calm down woman. Your man looking for you," Dalen told her. -

"What the fuck does he want?" She asked.

"For you to stop ignoring him. Go and talk him."

"You think it was right what he did to me?" Khloe asked. "That he would let a woman suck him off in front of me?" Dalen just shrugged.

"You were coming out ya mouth a lil heavy mama, so you kinda did deserve it," Dalen shrugged.

"That's complete bullshit. Of course you would agree with him."

"Just think about it like this. Would you rather him do it behind your back, or right to your face?"

"Don't make me slap the shit outta you," she sneered.

"I wouldn't do that if I were you," A female voice spoke up. Dalen looked up to see Sasha and Giselle standing behind Khloe. Dalen nearly dropped the bottle of water he was drinking as he stared at her.

"What in the hell you gonna do about it?" Khloe challenged. "You know you can't put your hands on me. And what the fuck are you doing here?"

"I don't gotta put my hands on you Khloe. I'll just suck Reign's dick." Khloe gasped audibly. "And don't worry bout what I'm doing here."

"Slut!" Khloe yelled. She marched off quickly. Sasha just rolled her eyes and shook her head.

"I thought you were the muscle. Why I gotta come to your rescue?" Sasha asked him. Dalen smiled at her.

"Every muscle has a weakness," he said looking

her up and down. She was wearing black leggings and a white crop top t-shirt, and he kept swallowing so he didn't end up drooling.

"I think I'm gonna start charging a fee whenever I gotta come to your rescue," she said.

"Really?" He chuckled. "What kind of fee?" He asked. Just as she was about to answer, Giselle groaned.

"How 'bout y'all stop flirting and fuck already? Damn. Is Reign here? He told me I was supposed to come see him."

"Giselle!" Sasha exclaimed, slapping her friend on the arm. "Why would you say that?" She whispered.

"Why the hell you think? Now stop acting up." Giselle looked at Dalen. "Dalen? Where's Reign?" Dalen coughed and patted his chest.

"He's um...he's in his office. Go on up but knock before you enter." Giselle walked off. Sasha stood there looking at Dalen. Their eyes locked as no words could form between them. He wanted to tell her that Giselle was right. He wanted to fuck her and he wanted to do that shit now, but he was worried about her. She must have been interested in him for Giselle to say that, but how interested was the question.

"She is right ya know," Sasha said. Dalen's mouth fell.

"Seriously?" he asked.

"Well yeah. I mean, we're adults right?" She said.

"True."

"But see, the thing is, I know of a situation where a man is sexy as all hell. Then when it came to the sex he had little to offer."

"Is that so?" Dalen asked.

"And I would hate to be disappointed."

"Come over here," Dalen ordered. She seemed shock by his demanding tone but it didn't scare her away. She walked over to him, standing in front of him. Dalen touched her dimple again and tucked his finger under her chin. He brought her lips up to his and he kissed her slightly. Sasha held her breath wishing he would come back for more. His mouth was soft against hers and she wanted more.

"More," she whispered. Dalen held the sides of

her face and kissed her fully. Her knees buckled. Damn she was not expecting that. Dalen held her up and kissed her. When she opened her mouth he gave her his tongue, tasting her sweetness. She moaned on his lips, kissing him back just as passionately. Just as Sasha went to wrap her arms around him, he broke off the kiss.

"What you doing?" Sasha asked out of breath.

"Take that as your sample, Dimple. Ain't no disappointments over here." Sasha just stared in shock not knowing what to do.

"Go on and practice," he said. He turned her around and patted her plump bottom softly. She yelped slightly as she walked away holding her bottom. She didn't have to worry about being disappointed. Dalen wouldn't leave an ounce of her body untouched.

Sasha caught up to Giselle on her way to Reign's office. She couldn't help touching her lips as the feeling of Dalen's lips tingled against hers. She was talking that shit because she figured maybe he would back off but he did the complete opposite. If he hadn't stopped kissing her, she would have been ready to climb his body and ride him right then and there.

"What's the matter with you?" Giselle asked Sasha.

"Dalen just kissed the shit out of me," Sasha sighed. Giselle smirked. She was happy for her friend but she also couldn't help but feel a little jealous. She just got kissed good, and Giselle, got a little ass kiss on the forehead last night like she was some child. That shit was beyond fucked up.

"How was that?" Giselle asked.

"I'm drunk off it," Sasha replied.

"Imagine if that man uses his dick."

"I don't even wanna think about it. Anyway, why you out here?" Sasha asked.

"I knocked he told me to wait," Giselle said. "I think Khloe is in there."

"That bitch is something else," Sasha said. Giselle's phone vibrated. She knew without even looking that it was Dean. After he left her house he'd been ringing off her phone. She was so pissed with him she couldn't even stand the thought of him at the moment. He had some nerve to really speak to her the way he did. Especially since he was dead wrong.

"What did he do now?" Sasha asked.

"I don't even want to talk about that man."

"Oh no, must have been serious." Giselle just shook her head and crossed her arms.

"I wish Reign would hurry up," Giselle groaned.

"Why it sound like you mad at him too?" Sasha asked.

"Cause I am," Giselle pouted.

"So what did he do?" Giselle shook her head again. She couldn't imagine the amount of embarrassment she'd feel if she told Sasha what he did to her. So she just opted to stay silent.

They waited in the hall for five more minutes before Reign opened the door. As usual when he saw her, his heart jumped. Today however she wouldn't make eye contact with him. Plus she looked pissed.

"Sorry to keep you waiting," he said, letting both the women in. Khloe sat up from her seat on his couch when she saw Sasha enter. Khloe really didn't like how much this woman was coming to see her man.

"Yeah, we were just fucking," Khloe stated.

Reign looked at her sharply.

"Well that must have been some whack fucking cause we ain't hear shit," Sasha challenged. Again, Khloe was speechless.

"First off," Reign said. "Don't be insulting my dick game, alright?" Sasha smiled at him. "And we weren't fucking. She just wants to make you jealous. In fact, we were arguing because she was ignoring me all damn night and all damn day." At that moment, Giselle's phone chose to vibrate. She cursed under her breath and picked up.

"I swear if you don't stop fucking calling me Dean, I'm gonna shove my foot so far up your fucking ass, you'll have toenails for teeth. Leave me the fuck alone until I'm ready to talk to you," Giselle gritted into the phone. She hung up before he could utter a word. Rolling her eyes, she took several deep breaths to calm herself before she returned to her business at hand. Only when she looked up everyone was staring at her. Reign was the most shocked.

"Wow," he said. Giselle shrugged.

"Get on my bad side if you want," she said

nonchalantly.

"Was that your man?" Reign asked.

"I honestly don't even know what the hell he is to me," Giselle said. Reign clenched his teeth. There was another man in her life. That relationship didn't seem to be working, but he had it in him to find out who the guy was and tell him Giselle was his. He was so surprised at himself for the thoughts running through his head. Instead of tonguing the woman down last night he kissed her on the damn forehead and now he was up here still thinking this woman was his? All while Khloe was sitting right across from him. That was his woman. Khloe was the one he was going to impregnate and marry eventually. Giselle was literally a dream and a fantasy that had no chance of happening.

"Anyway," Reign said, trying to keep his mind on the right thing. "Sasha I had a space set up for you in the dressing room. My apologies for how the women treated you." Sasha only nodded.

"I want you to start learning the routines immediately Sasha," Reign told her.

"I came here early today in hopes to learn them. I heard the girls talking about a practice but when I asked they played dumb, but I just showed up anyway," Sasha replied.

"If anyone gives you a problem Sash, just let me know. I will be sure to deal with them. Khloe please take Sasha and teach her the routines with the other women." Khloe couldn't believe Reign at the moment. The only thing stopping Khloe from speaking out was fear that he was going to pull another stunt like he did last night. There was no way she was going to give Sasha a chance to get remotely close to Reign. She didn't care what she had to do either. So Khloe stood and pretended like she was okay with what Reign told her to do. Sasha winked at Khloe before following her out of the office.

"You'll never touch him," Khloe whispered to Sasha. Either Sasha didn't hear the threat, or she didn't care because she didn't make any comment.

Watching Khloe and Sasha leave the office, Giselle felt almost afraid to be left alone with Reign. She was still upset by how he kissed her on the forehead. She probably didn't even have a good reason to be upset in the first place. The man had a whole girlfriend. A bitchy one, but still she was his.

"What did you want to talk about?" Giselle asked, ready to get this over with.

"Your work. If you are capable I'd like you to make some more outfits for the girls along with doing their makeup," Reign replied.

"I don't mind but I don't have a studio or a sewing machine at home. I wouldn't be able to do costumes unless I have the proper equipment."

"Not to worry I'll take care of it. I'll order the fabrics and equipment," he told her.

"That means I'll be here early and leaving late if I want to get work done. Making good outfits can take some time especially for every girl here," she said.

"That's also fine with me Giselle. Only problem is that I don't have any other rooms to give to you for your space. My utility closet over there however is big enough," he said pointing to a door in his office. "I can set up things there and it's all yours. You'll just have to share the office with me." Share the office, with him?

How much more of this man could she take? Could she handle being around him and watch him simply treat her like a child?

"Um, honestly Reign you think that's a good idea?" she asked.

"You're mad at me aren't you?" he asked her.

"What? How? Why would I be mad?" Giselle tried hard to play it off like she wasn't feeling some type of way.

"Because of what I did last night. Admit it," he ordered. Giselle sighed. She was caught.

"Okay, I'm mad," she admitted.

"I figured. You had a look in your eye." Giselle crossed her arms. "But, I apologize, little bit. I didn't meant to offend you with what I did."

"It's okay Reign." They looked at each other in silence for a moment. His dreads were splayed around his shoulders today. Her fingers itched to run her hands through them.

"Um, you understand fabrics?" She asked, to break to silence. "Because we can go through what to order."

"I know the basics but you're free to suggest anything. As a matter of fact, I want to know what else you can do. It seems you're very talented." Giselle shrugged.

"Not really," she shrugged. "I just like to learn things." One of his dreads fell in front of his face. He pushed it out of the way as he continued to look at her.

"But I can show you something else if you want to see," she offered.

"What is that?" he asked.

"Let me braid your dreads," she offered. His brows quirked.

"Braid it how?"

"Just two corn rolls, to keep it out of your face," she said.

"I don't see why not," he replied. Reign watched her walk over to him. His heart pumped in his chest hard as he realized she was about to touch him. He barely even let Khloe touch his hair but the need to feel her hands on him was too much.

"Actually, it would help if we used that stool," Giselle said, "The back of your chair is too high." He nodded, going over to sit on the stool next to his desk. He held his breath as she touched his shoulders then ran her fingers through his hair.

"Wow," she breathed. "You do a good job at maintaining these," she complimented. Reign couldn't answer just yet. He was mesmerized by the feeling of her hands.

Giselle sighed deeply. Why was this man so perfect? His hair smelled like coconut and cream and it was soft to the touch. She inhaled his scent then proceeded to braid his hair before he started wondering what was taking her so long.

"What made you decide to wear dreads?" She asked him.

"Actually I've always had dreads. My mother locked my hair the moment it was long enough and I never changed it."

"Did you ever ask her why?" Giselle asked. He chuckled.

"She said it reminded her of my father. He was shot and killed when I was little so I never really knew him that well. When I saw a photo I realized I did look like him so I kept my dreads. I thought that maybe if I reminded my mother of him she wouldn't be so lonely and unhappy about his passing." Giselle's heart clenched. Who knew he was that type of man.

"They don't look bad on you after all," she said.

"As they grew I just kept cutting them until they were shoulder length. I don't have time to deal with long ass hair." Giselle parted his hair in two and started on one braid.

"They are still amazing," she said. They fell silent as she continued to braid his hair. She wanted to take her time for the moment to last, but realistically she couldn't. She finished both corn rolls in 15 minutes.

"All done," she said. Without saying anything, he turned on the stool to face her. With him sitting down they were just about the same height. Again, their eyes were locked. She was waging a war within herself. Kiss him and possibly be embarrassed if he shunned her, or not kiss him and possibly miss out on the best kiss of her life. Giselle didn't know what to do.

"Thanks," he said softly. "You're one talented woman."

"I try," she smiled. Deciding to save herself from embarrassment, Giselle backed away from him. Reign cursed in his head when Giselle backed up. He had set it in his mind that he was going to make up for that stupid forehead kiss last night. Of course just before he went in for the kill, she backed away. He seriously needed to work on his game. He didn't have to try when it came to any of these women, or Khloe but Giselle was a different type of woman. Just his looks wasn't going to get him what he wanted. He had to do something more.

"Well, I'm gonna go watch the practice with the girls," he said.

"I think I'll join. Watching the routines may give me ideas for some new outfits," Giselle said. Reign nodded.

"That's a good idea," he said. Giselle touched his hair once more, letting her fingertips linger on the softness before she took her hand away and looked at him. Once more they were staring at each other. Both had so much to say but no words left their mouths. They were both victims of their own silence.

## Chapter Nine

Sasha stared at the other girls as they did their routine. No one wanted to show her the moves. She figured Khloe was behind all of it, telling the girls to be bitches, but Sasha paid her no mind. She watched them do the routine 3 times before she had the moves down pact in her head. No one knew she was a professional dancer and that helped her to remember the moves. Giselle was sitting by the bar looking on, taking notes in the notepad in her hand. She cheered Sasha on, telling her to get to the stage knowing Sasha already had the routine down especially since the girls wouldn't show her how to do the moves.

When their music stopped and the girls chatted with each other, Sasha cut in between them and started the song over again. When Maya's 'My love it like whoa', blared through the sound system, Sasha caught their attention. Winking at Khloe she replicated the moves they did, plus added her own. At that time she saw Reign enter the main room. He was looking at Giselle for a long time before he looked at Sasha. As she continued the dance he cheered her on, pleased at her moves. At the end she added a few flips and splits just to shove it in Khloe's face.

"You can't add that shit!" Khloe yelled, turning off the music. "Half of us can't even split!"

"That ain't my problem Khloe! You're the dancer aint you?!" Khloe tossed her the middle finger and walked away.

"Honestly Reign, what kind of fucking you been giving her? She's cranky as fuck!" Sasha exclaimed. Reign gasped in shock before he began laughing.

"I doubt my dick can cure her attitude," he said. Sasha looked at Dalen when she began thinking about dicks and fucking. When he winked at her she turned away from him quickly and took a deep breath. If she didn't control herself, she was the one that was going to get fucked.

The chefs from the kitchen came into the main room carrying platters of food for the dancers. Giselle put down her pad and came over to where Sasha stood.

"Show me some of those moves," she teased.

"If you really wanna know I can show you the flips." Sasha suggested. Giselle nodded.

Reign couldn't take his eyes off Giselle. Wherever she moved, his eyes followed her. As the other girls ate, he watched as Giselle went over to Sasha. They began talking and laughing with each other. Separating themselves from the other girls, Sasha performed another split. Giselle tied her curly hair into a bun. She took a deep breath and performed the split going down slowly until she was all the way down. Reign's eyes nearly popped out of his head as he watched her. Shutting his mouth before he drooled, Reign looked around to see if anyone was watching him. He caught Dalen looking right at him. The guard was standing at his post not moving a muscle.

Reign went over to him and stood next to him silently before speaking. He was trying to figure out what was the right thing to say at the moment. But in their silence, Reign looked at Dalen and realized the man was looking at the girls too. That jealousy egged at Reign when he thought about the fact that Dalen was watching Giselle like that. What in the world could he be thinking about her?

"She's a sight, isn't she?" Was all Reign could manage to say. Dalen grunted in response.

"I see the way you look at her," Dalen said.

"I can say the same for you," Reign shrugged.

"I've been single for a long time Reign. A girl like her ain't nothing average." Sasha was showing Giselle a cartwheel now. Her small body did the move with an expertise he didn't know she had.

Dalen looked at Reign briefly. Yeah, Reign was mesmerized by Sasha, Dalen could tell. He was trying to figure out what next to say to his brotha, but seeing Sasha in those small spandex shorts and sports bra kept dragging his attention away. Dancing was a crime for her, because she was damn near killing him with each move she made.

"Listen," Dalen said. "I know you want her. Trouble is, I want her too."

"Yeah I figured that," Reign replied. "I'm not ready to have no woman come in between us. That can never happen."

"True. And I think me and her sort of got a bond. I kissed the life outta her and she was all but ready to jump me." Reign glared at Dalen.

"When the fuck were you kissing her?" Reign asked. He didn't realize the tone he carried until Dalen gave him a look.

"Shit, sorry bro. I-I don't know where that came from," Reign shook his head.

"It was earlier. Just before she went up to your office," Dalen continued.

"Honestly, I shouldn't even be making any claims to anyone when I'm willingly keeping Khloe in my life. So I won't keep you from a woman you see a possible future with." Saying that burned his chest, but he wasn't going to hold no grudge against his brother.

"Should I even go there?" Dalen asked. He looked at Sasha again. This time she looked up at him as she rocked her hips.

"I don't see why you can't. But man, you're one lucky muthafucker. That woman is gorgeous," Reign said. Dalen kept his eyes on Sasha as she danced and joked around with Giselle. She did a booty pop and his balls throbbed.

"Fuck it," Dalen said throwing his hands up. He couldn't take it anymore.

"I think they're talking about us," Giselle whispered to Sasha. Reign and Dalen were glaring at them and whispering to each other.

"Don't bother me none," Sasha said, continuing to show her the dance moves.

"I guess but it makes me wonder what they talking about. Dalen is looking right at you," she said.

"Let me give him something to look at," Sasha smiled. She turned her back to Dalen and began popping her booty.

"Oh my god Sasha he's coming right after you!" Giselle laughed. "One tease too many!" Dalen charged up to them. He nodded to Giselle.

"Sorry for interrupting ladies. Sasha, come with me please," he said urgently.

"Where we going?" She asked.

"You can follow me dimples, or I can carry you." Sasha scoffed even though the look in his eyes were burning a hole through her head.

"I'd like to see you do that," she challenged. Dalen gave her an evil grin before picking her up by the waist and carrying her off. Giselle laughed at the pure shock on Sasha's face. She knew for a fact Dalen was about to give her friend some serious business.

Reign stared on in shock as Dalen carried Sasha away. He shook his head and tried to figure out what in the hell just happened. So, Dalen must have thought Reign was into Sasha, just like Reign thought Dalen was into Giselle. He was excited for his friend to have female company, but now he was fucking elated it wasn't his little beauty. Giselle watched her friend get carried off, then she turned and looked at Reign. They smiled at each other. Reign was a second away from going over to her when Khloe jumped onto him. He was surprised, but he held her weight in his arms.

"When was the last time we had some real alone time?" she asked. "Every time I turn around, Sasha is there nagging you."

"Cut that out Khloe. She's my new employee of course she's around a lot." Reign put her down. "And I asked you to show her the routine and you didn't. I need you to stop being a bitch to her and I mean it."

"Why the hell are you taking up for her so much?"

"Just chill out okay? I got work to do." Reign looked to where Giselle was standing but she was no longer there. Not seeing her in the main room he didn't know where she went and it would be awfully creepy if he followed her, so he just moved Khloe out of the way and began walking towards his office. He was not happy at the loss of his little beauty.

********

Dalen set Sasha in one of the private rooms of the club. She made no fuss or even said anything when he closed and locked the door behind him. When they looked at each other it was as if they spoke telepathically, because they both understood what they wanted and they didn't have to say any words. Sasha bit her bottom lip seductively. As Dalen walked towards her, she backed up teasingly. At the same time that he unbuttoned his jeans, she stuck her fingers in the side of her shorts getting ready to take them down.

When she raised a brow and her eyes flicked down to his groin, Dalen understood that she wanted to see what he was working with. Feeling confident, Dalen unzipped his pants, and pulled his dick out.

Sasha tried to hide her surprise at his dick but she didn't do a good job. In all honestly she wanted to make sure that what happened to Giselle wouldn't happen to her. Dalen was sexy as fuck but she had to make sure he would be satisfactory in the sack. But now looking at his dick his size was absolutely no problem at all. Her mouth was watering to suck him off, but they didn't have that much time. He was at work after all. Sasha pulled her shorts down, leaving them around her ankles. It was his turn to be shocked. He was determined that she was a African goddess reincarnated. And it was such a shame he wasn't going to get to savor the moment.

"You're so goddamn beautiful," he breathed. Sasha blushed and looked away from him for a minute.

"Come get it, my muscle," she teased. Dalen marched towards her. He grabbed her by the wrist and yanked her forward, kissing her lips hard. He didn't want to be too rough with her but she seemed to get even more turned on. After attacking her lips, Dalen pushed her onto the bed. He yanked off her shorts hanging from her ankle.

"Face down, ass up," he ordered her. She smiled devilishly at him and did was he said. When her ass was spread in front of him he had to hold his chest to see if he was going into cardiac arrest. Searching the night table drawer next to the bed, he found a large pack of condoms. Taking one out, he ripped it open with his teeth.

"What's taking you so long baby," she groaned swaying her hips. Dalen looked back at her to see the proof of her arousal dripping from her sweet canal and down her thighs. Dalen spanked her before grabbing onto her ass. She yelped in excitement at the feel of his hands on her. Securing the condom on his shaft, ran his tip along this entrance.

"Now, tell me how you want it," he demanded. "Because once I enter you baby, I don't think I will be able to take my time."

"Just fuck me," she groaned, trying to move her

hips to allow him to sink into her as he continued to rub her folds with his tip. That was all he needed to hear. Grabbing both of her cheeks, he slowly entered her. His breath was knocked out of him as her tight sheath surrounded him. He was only tip deep when he felt a slight resistance inside her. He waited for her to take a deep breath and arch her back some more before he began to slide into her again.

"Shit," she groaned grabbing onto the sheets. Dalen watched in awe as her pussy ate up his dick. "No more," she cried out, when he was halfway inside her. She reached back and pushed at his abdomen. Dalen listened to her. He moved his hands from her ass to her hips.

Sasha closed her eyes when she felt him pull out and surged back in. Her insides tingled as she could already feel an orgasm awakening within her. He was so thick and long Sasha never thought she would ever tell a man to stop halfway after putting in his dick. She was so wet, her juices were coating his dick and allowing him to move fluidly within her.

"You okay Dimples? He asked. Sasha could only

manage to nod. She felt his grip on her hips tighten and she knew just what that meant. Holding tight to the bed sheets, she gritted her teeth as he began slamming into her. He thrust into her as if he was searching for something until finally he thrust upwards. Sasha cried out as he hit her G-spot.

"Oh there it is," he teased, knowing he found the right spot. He grinded into her rhythmically, hitting her in the same spot each time with his tip. She couldn't believe she was about to come this fast. Her vibrating dildo didn't even make her come this fast. But she had to say, this is what she missed about sex with a man. The feel of his body hovering over hers and to hear his grunts and breathless curses only further enhanced her pleasure.

"I'm coming," she cried out trying to move away from his thrusts.

"Don't run," he ordered. "Take this shit." He lifted her hips in his hands, holding her off the bed so she couldn't move. She moaned and screamed into the bed. Even when she tried to move forward so he wasn't so deep inside her, he held her hips firm and brought her back down on his raging length. Her whole body went shock still as her orgasm poured from down her heart, through her stomach, and gushed out of her vagina. Her body felt like it was soaring as the feeling rushed over her.

Dalen watched in awe as Sasha's body shook. She dug her head into the mattress as she screamed. Dalen kept thrusting, loving the sound that her wet pussy made around his dick. Her muscles clenched and vibrated around him so much he was trying hard to not come but it was no use.

"You feel so good Dimples," he groaned, continuing to dig into her. Since she was soaking wet, he sunk his dick into her completely. Her muscles clenched him again and another stream of her cum coated him, that was his undoing. He thrust into her repeatedly as his balls clenched and released his release. He was so weak from the orgasm he dropped her hips. She plopped back onto the bed. Dalen fell forward, keeping himself up with his arms so he didn't fall on top of her back.

"Did I disappoint?" He whispered in her ear.

She pushed his arms from out under him making him fall onto her. They both began to laugh.

"Cocky bastard," she chuckled. He rolled off her as she turned onto her side. The laid there looking at each other for a moment.

"I have a confession," Sasha said. Dalen's heart began to pound.

"Please don't tell me you got a man!" He exclaimed. She laughed and kissed his chin.

"It's exactly the opposite actually."

"So what?"

"You're the first man I've been with for two years. I've um, I've just been really friendly with my vibrating dildo," she admitted.

"Wow, two years huh? No wonder you're so damn tight." She slapped his chest. "But seriously, why so long?" He asked. She thought deeply before answering.

"Because I didn't think I was good enough for another man. My ex...well let's just say it didn't turn out well. I saw the way you looked at me Dalen and all my desire to be with a man I thought was locked away came falling out of me."

"You're more than good enough for me Sasha. In fact, you're way too good for me and you don't even know it. Don't let any man make you feel like shit about yourself. You're gorgeous." Sasha smiled as a warm feeling bloomed in her heart. She started to question if this man was just a sexual conquest or was he going to be more than that to her. She was silently hoping that maybe he would be more than that. What they'd just shared was too powerful to just be a simple sexual conquest.

## Chapter Ten

"Relax your cheeks and sit still!" Giselle ordered Sasha for the tenth time. Ever since she came back from being with Dalen the woman wouldn't stop smiling and bouncing around. She continued to practice and then when they were just hanging around waiting until it was time to get dressed, she was texting constantly. Giselle caught a glimpse of one of the texts to see that it was Dalen. Giselle hadn't asked about the sex because it was obvious it was good. If it wasn't, Sasha wouldn't be so damn happy. Just before Giselle started doing makeup, he brought Sasha a plate of food and a piece of pie. Wasn't that nice of him? And now, Sasha wouldn't keep still so Giselle could do her job.

"Sorry girl!" Sasha said, putting her phone down. Giselle did her eyeshadow. But after hearing

Sasha's phone go off again Giselle gave in.

"Alright tell me! And don't spare the details! And what the fuck ya'll been talking about all night?" Sasha giggled then she just flat out started laughing.

"Okay, okay." She took a deep breath and told Giselle every single detail of what happened between them.

"Oh my god," was all Giselle could manage to say.

"Honestly Giselle, I-I haven't felt like this in a long time. Not since Jay," she admitted.

"Well, you deserve it. You're a gorgeous woman!" Giselle exclaimed. Sasha just sighed and blushed. Giselle was truly happy for her friend and just longed for the time when she would know what it was to feel just as happy as Sasha did.

"Now, quit all that smiling and bouncing around," Giselle teased. Sasha nodded her head and stayed still long enough to let Giselle work her magic.

All the girls let Giselle do their makeup for them and arrange some of their outfits. Hell, most of them actually talked to her. It was just Khloe that was being a bitch both to Giselle and Sasha. For some reason it was as if Khloe had a grudge against Sasha and no one knew why.

"Perfect. You all look stunning," Reign said, approving all of the girls. "Giselle wonderful job." Giselle could only beam in happiness as he accepted her work. When all the girls went off to make final preparations before the doors to the club opened, Reign stopped Sasha.

"You got an extra glow to ya," he said to her. "I wonder what the hell got you so happy," he teased. Giselle tried to hide her laughter as Sasha blushed in embarrassment.

"Stop it Reign," Sasha giggled. "You know what happened!" Reign smiled and threw his arm around her shoulder.

"Look, what is it he calls you? Dimples?" Reign asked.

"Hey you're not allowed to call me that!" Sasha exclaimed. "Only my muscle can call me that."

"Oh excuse the hell outta us," Giselle smiled.

"Anyway," Reign continued. "Dalen is my boy.

So I'll make sure to look out for his woman when he can't."

"Thanks," She smiled. "I appreciate that." Just as Reign took his arm from around Sasha, Dalen approached.

"We're gonna get ready!" Sasha said, grabbing Giselle and leading her away. That left Reign and Dalen alone.

"Don't look so sour," Reign told him.

"I thought you told me she was all mine," Dalen said.

"I did," Reign nodded.

"So what the hell you flirting with her for Reign? The woman is-"

"Calm down!" Reign exclaimed. "Earlier we were both confused. I thought you wanted Giselle, and you thought I wanted Sasha. I don't want Sasha bro, I was talking about Giselle." Dalen gasped. It took him only a minute to put two and two together.

"Oh I see. Wait, you like Giselle. Is that why you asked me what I thought of her?" Reign nodded. "Well, I mean why don't you just go get here then?" Reign just shrugged.

"I don't know if it'll work out with me like it worked out with you. But don't worry, I wasn't flirting with your girl. I just told her I have her back cause you're my boy." Dalen smiled and patted his friend on the back.

"This one, she's a different kind of woman," Dalen said. "A real different kind." Reign knew from the words that left Dalen's mouth and the look in his eyes that Dalen was about to embark on something new and special in his life. For what that man has been through, Reign knew Dalen deserved something special for once. Reign looked towards the direction the women had went off into. Instead of Giselle though, he saw Khloe was standing there watching everything that had just went down. She looked directly at Reign her expression one of anger. He really didn't know what the hell he was doing. Especially when it came to Khloe.

Khloe watched as Giselle and Sasha walked to the dressing room smiling and laughing. She'd watched the whole time as Reign was openly flirting with that bitch Sasha like Khloe didn't exist. Reign was still upset at her for what she said but this was taking it too far. If he wanted to be with other women so blatantly in her face, she had no problem with that. Two could definitely play that game. When Reign had looked at her Khloe had tried to depict her sadness and betrayal on her face so he knew he had fucked up. He just stared back at her and said absolutely nothing. Khloe wasn't sure what the hell was going on in his head but she was very sure she was not about to let him treat her like shit all for some new bitch. Reign never knew what it was to potentially lose Khloe. Maybe that's why he acted the way he did. It was time for Khloe to play as many games as Reign was playing. She just needed to find a new player to add to the game.

Dean watched from down the street as the lights came on in the club as they opened for the night. He'd been calling Giselle all damn day and she refused to talk to him. He understood why she would mad but he found it incredibly immature that she would be ignoring him. So after he calmed himself down, he went back to her house to find that she was gone. He came straight to the strip club and caught her in time to see her entering the building. He hated the fact that she would be there all day, and he was going to go in there and forcefully remove her. He didn't understand the scope of the place and he saw the guards posted out front. No doubt if he went trying to barge inside there was going to be a big scene and he didn't want to go out like that. So he decided he'd wait for her to leave the club and then he'd confront her in person.

Only problem with that plan was that she never left the building. Once the lights cut on in the club Dean realized she was in there all damn day and probably wasn't going to leave until the place closed for the night again.

"Son of a bitch," he snapped as he stomped his way out of his car. He slammed the door and marched towards the club. So he guess he just had to go in there and get her out himself.

Dean paid the fee to get into the building then waited to get patted down by security. He thought this was going to be a one shot deal and he was probably going to catch Giselle on the stage or in front of some man shaking her ass but he didn't see any sign of her. All he did see was random women dressed exotically that kept garnering his attention. After 15 minutes of searching the joint, he hadn't seen a glimpse of Giselle but had turned down three offers for dances. Not knowing what else to do in the time being before he figured out where Giselle was, he went to the bar and ordered himself a drink. He hadn't even taken two sips of his jack and coke when a pair of small hands caressed his shoulders. He looked up to see a tall slender woman with large breasts cozying up to him.

"All alone?" she asked. Dean was going to dismiss her when she licked her full lips. He took a good look at her body and smiled at her. Giselle was acting like a child and putting him through this wild goose chase in the first place. No sense in him turning down another dance or something more from someone amazing sexy who was willing to give him a good time.

"For now I am," Dean answered.

"So then let me accompany you." When she ran

her hands across his chest, his penis hardened. Like he had told Giselle earlier, she wasn't doing that great a job at keeping him satisfied. Maybe she would learn her lesson if he fucked another woman to prove his point. He needed to get his pleasure when he wanted, and her making him wait was going to make him find someone else.

"I don't want no regular old company," Dean said. He took her hand and let her feel his arousal. She licked her lips again.

"That's the exact kind of company I'm looking to give," she smiled. Dean finished his drink in one gulp and allowed her to lead him away to a private room. When they entered the room and she closed the door, Dean kicked off his shoes and jeans and hopped onto the mattress. She straddled his hips and pulled off the bikini top she was wearing. Dean grabbed a fistful of her full breasts.

"What's your name?" He asked her.

"Khloe," she smiled.

"I wonder what a pretty little thing like you is doing working at a strip club."

"I ask myself that all the time," she said. "I hope you like a woman on top, because I love to ride."

Khloe fell on top of Dean in a heap. She hadn't been keeping track of time so she had no idea how long they'd been in the room fucking, but she was determined not to leave until she was good and ready. The first thing she noticed with Dean however was that Reign definitely had the bigger dick. Sometimes though you weren't always going to find a big dick. You just had to work with what you had. Khloe needed to find what turned Dean on the most and that's where she was going to benefit from having sex with him in the first place.

She found out that there was an aggression inside of him that he seemed to be suppressing. Khloe noticed that when he reached for her neck as he fucked her, he immediately pulled back. Khloe took his hand and put it back around her neck. He recognized what she was allowing him to do, and since then he fucked Khloe like there was no tomorrow. He choked her, pulled her hair to the edge of pain and he wasn't shy about spanking her. After riding him relentlessly, they'd both come at the same time, exhausted and satisfied.

"I wasn't expecting that tonight," he said, pulling on his jeans. Khloe smiled as she redressed.

"Actually me either. But I am glad we did do it."

"Yeah me too." Dean fetched his wallet to pay her. Even though he was going to build a life with Giselle, he knew he couldn't have sex with her like he wanted to. She was just too damn soft. Being able to abuse Khloe's body opened him up to the possibility that he could always turn to her when he needed the release Giselle wouldn't give him. Khloe was perfect for him.

"I don't know about your rules Khloe, but I'd love to have your number. I don't think if I came back here I would want to be with any other woman," he said. Khloe smiled.

"Yeah...yeah you can have my number." Since

she wasn't carrying her phone, she gave him her number. She didn't know what kind of water she was treading by keeping in contact with this man but she didn't care. When they left the room, unlike any man she'd been with, he actually kissed her passionately, then he kissed her softly on the cheek. Reign sometimes didn't even show her that much passion. She just figured that was just because that was just the type of man Reign was.

"I'll keep in touch Khloe." He smiled at her then walked away. He was going to wait for Giselle, but all that anger that he had wound up in him with her disappeared the moment he had an orgasm. Khloe had let him do any and everything to her body and he was beyond sated. Feeling light on his feet, he whistled and walked towards the exit of the club. Dean could wait until Giselle got home to talk with her. Right now, he wanted to bask in his orgasm high. He was just thankful he came into the club in the first place. If he hadn't he would have never came across the magnificence of Khloe.

********

Giselle watched as Reign looked through the outfits she'd sketched. She wasn't even a good illustrator but he insisted on her showing what she had. When the club got into full swing for the night, Reign and Giselle had been arranging the utility closet to be ready when the fabrics and sewing machine arrived. Giselle didn't even know why it was called a closet in the first place. It was just as large as any normal office and that was just a testament as to how large, Reign's office was. Giselle was nervous and twitchy as she continued to watch him go through the drawings.

"I like them," he said. "You still amaze me."

"It ain't no big deal." She shrugged. Sighing she ran her hands through her hair.

"You look exhausted," he said.

"Yeah I am, sort of. Didn't really sleep as much as I wanted last night and I've been here all day practically." The club was almost close to closing so they would all be able to leave and get home soon.

"So go on home then, I won't keep you," he suggested. Reign was just about to offer to take Giselle home when his office door opened and Khloe appeared. Damn, it was like every time he thought about making his move, Khloe appeared.

"Dismissed," Khloe snapped at Giselle. Giselle looked her up and down before shaking her head. Honestly, Giselle knew she could whoop Khloe's ass easily especially with her kickboxing skills. It was probably why she just let Khloe think she was the shit.

"I do not have the energy for you," Giselle mumbled. "Good night Reign."

"Goodnight Giselle," he said to her. When the door closed behind her he looked at Khloe.

"Why you treat her like that?" Reign asked Khloe.

"Because I can," Khloe replied.

"One day you're going to regret talking to people the way you do Khloe." Khloe just shrugged at his words. She really didn't care or think anyone would ever step to her.

"By the way, where you been all night? I haven't really seen you," Reign said.

"I been busy," Khloe said, dismissing him easily. Reign got the idea that she was still upset at him because he let Ginger suck him off.

"Are you still mad at me? Because you know I can make it up to you." Khloe hesitated for a moment. The relationship she had with Reign was an open one, or so he claimed. Which meant they were involved with each other but they were not exclusive. Technically they could fuck around with whoever they wanted to but because they didn't wear protection most times, Reign's number one rule was that the both of them be completely honest about who they fucked and when they fucked. Yet still, Khloe didn't want to tell Reign any of what she'd been through with Dean. Not until she would completely reap the benefits of having him fear losing her. What she knew for sure though was that after that workout Dean gave her, her pussy was sore. There was no way she was about to handle Reign too.

"I'm not mad Reign, but I am tired. I don't got the energy for any making up," she said instead. Reign nodded.

"No problem. But you gotta catch up on your sleep," he told her.

"I will. Just wished I had someone to fall asleep with tonight," she said in an effort to suggest that she wanted to finally be invited over to his home. She didn't know where he lived but she just had a feeling the place was luxurious as all hell.

"Fine, I'll stay the night with you," he replied. Khloe rolled her eyes. That was so not what she was going for.

"You know, any other man would be happy to invite me to their home and have me as their exclusive girlfriend and partner. They wouldn't hide shit from me," she decided to say as a way to alert him that he could lose her if he didn't change his ways. Instead of it going the way she thought it would however, it went the complete opposite way.

"Sounds like you're threatening me," he said.

"Take it how you want," she shrugged.

"If you're not satisfied with me Khloe I'm not keeping you in this relationship with me, or whatever it is we have. You can easily back out of it and that would be it." Khloe was stunned into silence as she realized her sleeping with another man wasn't going to make

Reign fearful of losing her. It was only going to give him a reason to officially end what they had going on. Maybe it would even push him away into the arms of another woman. Possibly Sasha. Khloe couldn't let that happen. Fuck. Reign wasn't allowed to know she had relations with another man. It would be the end of them.

# Chapter Twelve

When Giselle finally parked in front of her house, she sighed. Today was a long ass day, and she couldn't even imagine how long it was going to keep being as she continued to work there. What made it harder was working right next to Reign and not be able to do anything with him. That in itself was tiring too. Giselle got out of her car and walked up her walkway. A shadow moved from somewhere next to her house and she quickly put a finger on the mace she carried around her keychain.

"Who's there?" She called out. "You can hide all you want but if you sneak up on me I will hurt you!" A familiar chuckle sounded and Dean came from behind the house.

"How in the hell a small woman like you gonna hurt me?" He joked. Giselle sighed and her eyes.

"What the fuck you doing out here?" She asked. "It's almost five in the morning."

"I decided to wait for you. I mean that's what a man is supposed to do right? Wait hand and foot for his woman?"

"I am not your woman," she groaned going to her door and unlocking it. He followed her inside and closed the door.

"Yeah, yeah, but technically you are. Anyways, that doesn't matter." Giselle just sighed and let him think what he wanted. She didn't have the energy to be angry or to argue with him. All she wanted was some sleep. Dean followed her up to her bedroom. She was so tired she plopped down into the bed without event taking her clothes off.

"That place sure seems hard to work in," Dean said taking off her shoes. Giselle just nodded and let him undress her. When she was naked he went into the bathroom and turned on the shower. She got up reluctantly and went to the bathroom. He sat on the toilet while she took her shower.

"Look. I think I need to apologize for earlier. I

was out of line," Dean sighed.

"Damn right you were," Giselle huffed.

"I was just kind of jealous," he admitted. Giselle turned off the shower and opened the curtain. She stared at him softly.

"Jealous for what?" She asked. He shrugged and stood, holding a towel open for her.

"Just jealous of whoever was getting your time," he said.

"I was working Dean. No one was getting my time but the people I work for in order to pay my bills," she replied.

"Which I don't understand. Because I can take care of you and we can just be together. I'm not really sure why you playing all these games," Dean said.

"I don't want to be committed Dean, that's as simple as it is. If we're going to be together we need to build on a relationship first. And honestly with the way you been acting, it's not been looking too good. So I don't see any rush to get into a commitment we both don't seem ready for."

Dean helped her dry off before they both left the

bathroom. She slipped into another one of her nighties and got into bed. This whole relationship conversation was not one she wanted to have at the moment.

"Are you leaving?" She asked him softly.

"If you want me to," he said. Giselle thought for a moment.

"No, I want you to stay." He nodded and undressed, leaving on his boxers. Turning out the lights he climbed into bed with her. He put an arm around her and drew her close. Giselle would have loved to be in Reign's arms. She could just imagine how good it would feel. But at the moment, she just had Dean. And as sad as it was, she would rather be in Dean's arms than to be alone.

********

"Hey," Dalen said as Reign entered his room early the next morning. Dalen was surprised that after a long night at the club, Reign was back again after only a couple of hours. Talk about dedicated. Reign never took days off, and he was always at the club no matter how late he stayed the night before.

"What's up?" Reign questioned, wondering why

Dalen called him up here. "And where the fuck you going?" Reign smiled, seeing Dalen in a pair of jeans and a black button up. Dalen flipped him the bird.

"Man, pussy sure does change a man," Reign continued to tease.

"You wouldn't know that, would you? Because I've yet to see you change after being with Khloe for so long." Reign had to agree to that one.

"Yeah true that. Anyway what's up? I gotta get ready for a meeting."

"Right. Look I hate to ask but um, me and Sasha was speaking all night when she got home last night. Stupidly I told her that I would pick her up and take her for breakfast today," Dalen said. Reign knew immediately what his friend was asking for.

"No worries," Reign said. He dug into his pocket and threw Dalen the keys to his BMW. He always left it parked in the parking lot of the club just in case Dalen would need it.

"One day I'll get my shit together," Dalen sighed.

"If my mom never bought this place then I

would be just like you. Trying to make it anyway I can. So don't be ashamed of what you gotta do until you get your shit together. And really, you have your shit together more than I do. Money doesn't make you more of a man," Reign said.

"I appreciate that," Dalen smiled.

"Now. I think you should take her to that place on sunrise. They got good food and the perfect scenery for a midafternoon fucking." Dalen threw the TV remote control at Reign. Reign ducked and laughed.

"Don't talk about my Sasha like that," Dalen laughed.

"You got it," Reign said backing out of the room. "My apologies to your Sasha." When the door closed, Dalen thought about what he just said. He called the woman his. She may not know it yet, but his gut was telling him she was more than a one night stand.

Was this a date? Sasha didn't know, but he asked her to breakfast. He said he would pick her up too. So this was a date? She was relieved that this man actually kept talking to her after she gave up her goods.

In fact, he didn't treat her any different because they'd already had sex. She was really feeling this man.

When Dalen beeped the car horn, Sasha came out of her house immediately. He was shocked she was actually punctual. He was more delighted to see her in a yellow sundress, with nude wedge heels. She looked gorgeous.

"Hey Dimples," he greeted, when he got out of the car to open the car door for her. She kissed his lips lightly in greeting.

"You look beautiful," he said.

"Thank you," she smiled.

As they drove out to the seaside diner, Dalen couldn't help but think about doing this with this woman every day. In his head he could see himself waking up to her, falling asleep with her, and taking care of her. He couldn't even understand how he was feeling like this after so little time, but it was happening and he didn't desire to change it. Sometimes the heart just knew what it wanted.

"So why exotic dancing?" Dalen asked her as they sat down to eat.

"It's a dance that I haven't done before. Or well, I do it but in my house when no one is watching. I'm a professional dancer so I love every aspect of dance. And dancing for Reign, well it will bring a steady check so I thought it was a good deal."

"Yeah you dance different from most of the girls. They have to take their clothes off to get money. So far you haven't flaunted your boobs and men are raving after you."

"Yeah, I don't mind the dancing but the stripping…well we'll see if I get into that."

"Hm, don't get into it," Dalen said.

"Why?" She asked. "Want it all to yourself?"

"I sure as hell do," he admitted. Sasha couldn't help to blush as she sipped her mimosa.

"So um, Reign told me that he would look out for me when I needed it. He said you were his boy. I have a feeling that you two are really close," Sasha changed the subject.

"That's my brother right there. Ain't nothing we won't do for each other."

"That's just like me and Giselle. She's more than

just my best friend."

"When you don't got family, friendships are important," Dalen said.

"I guess we have that in common. No family but our best friends." Sasha raised her glass. "Cheers to that," she smiled. He knocked her glass with his as they toasted.

After their brunch, they walked along the boardwalk taking in the sights. He loved talking to her. There was nothing sexual about their time together and he found he was still intrigued by her. She was intelligent, funny and he could tell she had a big heart. Pair that with her amazing body and sexual appetite, she was the perfect woman for Dalen.

"The breeze is a little chilly," Sasha said, as they sat on a bench on the board walk. He pulled her close to him and kept an arm around her. Sasha of course wasn't cold. She just wanted to get close to the man. She turned her head and kissed him on the neck. When he shivered, Sasha smiled and continued to kiss his neck. She nibbled, licked, and kissed his neck repeatedly until he groaned.

She captured his lips in a sweet kiss. He held her face and kissed her back. He wasn't shy about kissing her deeply in public and she was beginning to feel the effects of his sweet kisses. Her insides were clenching and crying out for something more.

"Dalen," she moaned.

"Look what you started," he said, putting her hand against his rock hard length.

"Well let's finish it," she challenged. When they looked at each other, something just clicked and they both knew what they wanted to do. Getting up, Dalen took her hand and led her away. They went back to the car. Sasha didn't know where they were gonna go, but once in the car, he drove off quickly. Driving for five minutes, he pulled into a vacant parking lot away from the crowd of the boardwalk. He opened the car door for her again and led her towards the boardwalk before they went down under it.

"You're so kinky I love it," Sasha giggled.

"Come here girl," he smiled. He put her against one of the wooden beams and unzipped his jeans. She hiked up her dress, as he approached her. He picked her up, holding her steady and wrapping her legs around his waist. Feeling for her underwear, he slid them to the side.

"Wait!" She exclaimed. "You gotta put a condom on!"

"Shit!" He'd nearly forgotten about that part. His mind was wrapped up in the web of lust to think clearly. He reached into his back pocket for his wallet. He was thankful he had a condom in there. Sasha kissed his neck as he put the condom on. He couldn't get the condom on fast enough. He just had to be inside her. He pushed his tip inside her to get a feeling of how wet she was. She was practically dripping.

"Damn baby," he moaned, kissing her neck. He clutched her thigh as he thrust his whole length into her. She cried out, clawing at his shoulders.

"Oh fuck," she whispered, digging her head into his chest. He pumped her at a steady pace. Over the sounds of the water from the beach crashing along the large rocks at the shore, her short breathy moans sounded in his ear and vibrated all the way to his heart. He could hear the gushing sounds of her impending release.

"Come for me baby," he moaned. He drilled the inside of her as she began grinding against him. Her moans were almost screams of passion. Dalen felt as her muscles clenched when she came hard. Her legs clamped tight around him as her body went into spasms. He grunted and shouted in his own pleasure as he gave one last thrust. He came violently himself. He was so weak from it, his own knees gave out and the both of them fell to the ground. Dalen held Sasha tight so he would take the brunt of the fall. They both laughed and held onto each other.

"Whew," she gasped. "I gotta stop coming so hard for you. You're gonna get cocky." Dalen ran a hand through her straight hair.

"I won't get cocky," he said. "I'll just keep giving you cock." She began to laugh uncontrollably. Dalen just held onto her and closed his eyes, savoring the sound of her sweet laughter.

********

In the early hours of the day, the club was closed for business, but Reign was sitting in his office with a potential client.

"When do you want the party to take place?" Reign asked her. The woman wanted to throw a huge masquerade party. Reign hardly ever rented out his place for parties, but this woman was bringing in new clients, and paying him a lot of money.

"In a month," she said. "I'm turning 30."

"Congratulations," Reign said. "So, are you going to hire a decorator? A caterer? Or a bartender or would you like to use what we already have here at the club?"

"I was actually anticipating using your resources here. I'm not sure however if you have a decorator to put on to work. But if you do then I would greatly appreciate that. A lot of people rave about coming here that's why I want my party to be here. And I'm ready to pay the price for the venue, the food, the bar, and even the dancers." Reign nodded.

"Okay then. Tell me what you want and I will make it happen." He opened his planner and wrote down everything the woman said. Even though it was going to be a lot to plan in such a short time, he wasn't going to miss this opportunity to make some serious money.

"We'll keep in touch while I plan everything, thank you Tamar." She clapped in happiness and shook his hand. When Tamar left, he went over his notes to make sure he understood what the woman wanted and just what he was going to have to do. He was thinking that he couldn't do this all on his own when a knock came to his door.

"Come in," he called out. Giselle walked in, bringing in her bright smile and luscious vanilla scent.

"Hey," she greeted. "Thought I would start early," she said.

"It's no problem. In fact, I could use your help actually. Are you good at party planning?" When she smiled even brighter, Reign just handed her the notes he took. She looked at the notes and studied them. Reign could only admire her beautiful profile as she concentrated.

"Okay well, I can help you plan this of course. And if you want the women to have new outfits to match the theme I can do that too. Plus makeup for that night," she said.

"I don't want to put to much pressure on you Giselle, it may be a lot," he told her.

"I'm a tough cookie, I can handle it," she smiled.

"I like to hear that. I got some of the fabrics here, but I'm still waiting for the sewing machine. You can check it out in the room there." Giselle nodded and went to the room. She was in love with all the fabrics. She never considered herself to be a fashion designer but she liked to make things and with this new high end fabric she was excited to get started. When she looked at Reign he was already looking at her. He smiled and looked away getting back to his job. Giselle did the same, deciding to sort through the fabrics and then go measure all the girls. Today she came here alone because Miss Sasha was with Dalen all morning, probably getting her groove on. Giselle had to be happy for her friend, it was a long time coming and she deserved to be happy. Sadly, Giselle couldn't say the same for herself. She had a lot of work to do in a matter of a month to get a party planned and that should surely take her mind off the burning heat she felt around Reign, and the jealousy she felt at not being able to have what her friend did. For now, Giselle just needed to put her head down and just work. Maybe that would blur out anything wrong in her life at the moment.

# Chapter Thirteen

The headboard slammed against the wall as Dean fucked Khloe into the mattress. How many times had they been in this position? How many times was he fucking her amazing body? After a couple weeks, Dean lost track of time. All he knew was that he had stopped putting up with Giselle not offering him that much of her time, and looking towards Khloe for his pleasure. That was working out perfectly for him.

Dean choked Khloe tightly until she came apart on his dick. He went right with her, jerking as he released his load inside her. She gasped loudly.

"You came in me!" She yelled, hitting him on the chest.

"Damn it, sorry baby. You know you feel so damn good!" Khloe couldn't really be angry at that. She knew she felt good. Of course he would find it hard not to come inside her.

"You lucky I like you so much," she smiled. Dean kissed her on the mouth and helped her up from the bed.

"Come, let me drop you back to the club," he said. It was midafternoon and he knew she had to get work done before the club opened. Unlike Giselle, Khloe was willing to risk a little bit of her time to be with Dean.

"Do you have a woman Dean?" She asked as she began getting dressed. Dean felt no reason to lie to her.

"I do. But she's not really satisfying me as much as you do babe." Khloe just nodded. She was actually fine with that because then she wouldn't have to try and juggle another relationship. She just wanted Dean for the sex when Reign wasn't giving her attention.

"We don't have to be together Dean. But I like having sex with you. So the level we're on right now is perfect for me," Khloe said.

"And it's perfect for me. I like having sex with you too," he agreed. Khloe kissed him and continued to get dressed. Good sex, no strings attached. Yes, it was perfect.

When Dean dropped Khloe off at the club, she kissed him on the cheek and immediately hopped out of the car. She bumped into Dalen upon entering. Dalen gave her a look but didn't say anything to her. Khloe rolled her eyes at him and went straight up to Reign's office. He was on the phone with someone speaking rapidly when she entered. He smiled at her but kept with his phone call. She had only had sex with Dean to sort of get back at Reign, but she chickened out and didn't even want to tell Reign what she did. And then she kept going back to Dean to have sex. Just something about it intrigued her. Dean had an appetite that was relentless and Khloe didn't mind sating him. But that meant her sexual relationship with Reign dwindled. She couldn't handle both men and it was a sacrifice.

"Where you been?" Reign asked her.

"Nowhere," she replied. He sat in his chair and looked at her. Reign was a very intuitive man and he loved to observe. She got restless as he just stared at her. She was already figuring that he knew she'd been having sex with another man. And it wasn't like she was cheating or something. They had this open relationship for a reason.

"You've been nowhere a lot lately," he said. When he continued to stare Khloe just rolled her eyes.

"Where's your newbie?" she asked speaking of Sasha. "I'm surprised she ain't in here riding your dick." The thought of Giselle riding his dick made his whole body shiver. He didn't know why Khloe felt the need to mention another female but he wasn't going to let it slide. Khloe was being a drama queen so he just decided to play along with it.

"Well, she wanted to ride my dick but I told her no. On account that I've been waiting for you. My dick is still not getting rode so I guess I'll call her back in here and she can ride me."

"She asked to ride you?" Khloe asked. Reign didn't answer. "And you would let her do it wouldn't you?"

"I don't see why not," he shrugged.

"You know what," Khloe snapped standing up. "I've never forgiven you for making that bitch suck you off in front of me. So make that hoe ride you. Just know that I've been getting fucked daily and surely not by you." Reign's eyes widened. He was shocked to hear that she was having sex with someone but he wasn't mad. In fact he appreciated she was telling him the truth.

"Interesting," he said.

"You damn right it is," she huffed.

"It's no problem Khloe you can do whatever you want. Has he been wearing a condom?" Reign asked.

"Of course he has," she lied. "You're the only man I would ever let inside me unprotected."

"Fine." Reign ended the conversation right there, not having much else to say. He continued to write up receipts for Tamar so she knew everything she was being charged for. Her party was coming up this weekend. He'd never planned something in short notice and now that it was coming near, he was finally able to take a breather. For the weeks until her party, he worked hard day and night to pull it off. In hindsight he should have charged her extra for booking him so last minute.

"You look tired," Khloe said after she calmed down. She sat back down, feeling lighter about having just telling him the truth. It did kind of hurt though that he wasn't even upset. It didn't even seem like he cared she was fucking someone else. She secretly began to fear that he was already plotting a way to sleep with Sasha to get back at her.

"Yeah a little," he answered her. "I've been staying late with this project."

"Sorry I haven't really been paying attention to you," she said trying to show him that she still cared about him and in no means was trying to end whatever they had.

"You're allowed to have a life Khloe. That's why we're in the relationship we are in now."

"I guess so. But um, there's some things that I miss doing with you. And I shouldn't have been neglecting you. Seeing you this stressed I wanna give you some relieve to get you relaxed." When she licked her lips, Reign knew exactly what she was talking about.

Khloe didn't wait for him to give her permission. She flipped her hair over her shoulders and strutted towards him. He was silent as she got into her favorite position behind his desk and unzipped his pants. With a shrug, Reign put his hands behind his head and let her have full control. She slowly licked him from base to tip, gliding her tongue around his tip before sinking it into her mouth. He groaned and sat back, letting his head fall back. Damn, he didn't know how much he really needed this. He could feel the tension in his body begin to melt away as pleasure crept in. Unlike before, she didn't play any games or try to act like the world's greatest porn star. She simply sucked his dick fluidly, swallowing him as deep as she could. She popped him out of her mouth and sucked his balls. He choked on his own tongue as he gasped in pleasure.

"Wow Khloe," he breathed. "Keep doing that." Just as the words came from his mouth the crackle of the intercom in his room sounded. Sasha's voice came sounding over the intercom.

"Reign come down to the main room right now!" She sounded urgent. Reign sat forward and took Khloe from his dick.

"What happened?" He asked back to Sasha. She didn't respond. "Shit," he cursed. He stood and began tucking himself back into his pants.

"Wait you're leaving?" She stammered. "What for? Let the guards handle it!"

"Just wait here Khloe, okay? Let me see what's up with Sasha." He buttoned his jeans and darted out of the room. Khloe punched the ground in anger. Here she was, her mouth full of his balls and he was ditching her to go look after another woman! Khloe felt stupid because she had just admitted she was sleeping with another man in anger towards Reign. She tried to make it up to him to show she was still very interested in being with him but then he just jumps up to run to the next bitch. Khloe was seriously getting tired of Sasha trying to scheme her way into Reign's life. There was probably nothing wrong with the slut in the first place she just wanted fucking attention. First the flirting, then trying to have sex with him, and now trying to pull his attention? Sasha was doing too fucking much. Of course Reign was falling for it easily. Can you believe it?

********

Giselle felt steam coming out of her ears as she drove to work angrily. For one, she was late, and two she was starving. Dean had called her repeatedly telling her that he wanted to take her out and spend time with her. Giselle was hesitant because she was exhausted but she knew she'd been neglecting him and thought he deserved better. So she was ready to give him her time and the fucker was a no show. Giselle had spent her whole morning waiting for him, so she hadn't eaten and now she was paying the price for that with her rumbling stomach. Walking into the club she knew she appeared gruff because no one looked at her or even bothered her. In the ladies dressing room, Giselle was busy trying to measure the women to get their outfits perfect for the masquerade party that was coming up soon.

Her phone was vibrating repeatedly with Dean's

number popping up. Giselle just kept looking at it and rolling her eyes not even bothering to pay him any attention. Dean's most famous act was calling her repeatedly after he'd fucked up. Like he couldn't take the hint that she needed time to calm the hell down, especially since he played her by leaving her hanging in the first place. After his tenth call, Giselle cursed and sucked her teeth. She went into the corner of the dressing room and answered.

"What?" she snapped.

"Giselle I am so-" Giselle cut him off.

"Where the hell were you?" she snapped at him.

"Sorry baby I got tied up! One of my trainee's got into a fight and I had to handle it!" Dean had to think quick about the excuse to give her. Even though Giselle wasn't trying to claim him he knew he would completely lose her if he admitted he was busy fucking another woman and that made him miss their date. In fact, he had completely forgotten about it until he dropped Khloe  back off at the club and saw Giselle's car parked up in the parking lot.

"You could have called me," Giselle said into the

phone. "Just like you can blow my phone up now, you could have damn well called me before."

"Look, just come outside okay? I'm in front of the club. I brought you something," he said.

"What the fuck are you doing here?" She asked. She was very uncomfortable with the idea that he would just pull up at her place of work.

"How you just gonna show up and not even tell me you were coming?!" she asked.

"Stay put," she ordered. "I'm coming outside." Giselle hung up the phone and stormed out of the dressing room.

"Where you going?" Sasha asked when Giselle stormed past her.

"Dean is outside!" Giselle exclaimed. Sasha didn't understand why her friend was so upset, but she followed Giselle in case anything went wrong.

When they approached the front door, Sasha looked around for Dalen but he wasn't in sight. Last time they'd spoken he'd dropped her off to the club after another early afternoon date and said he was gonna go home to get something and to change his clothes. Sasha guessed he just wasn't back yet. She followed behind Giselle quietly who marched up to Dean.

"You need to go home," Giselle told him. She didn't even give notice to the flowers he was carrying. Giselle just point blank didn't care about that apology.

"Let me just take you to eat right now," he said. "I know you must be hungry."

"Well yeah I'm hungry because of you! But I'm fine I can take care of myself. You're always dogging me about not making time for you and when I do, you come up with some bullshit ass excuse about why you was a no show. Forget about it Dean. Just...just go home. We can talk later."

"Come on Giselle, get in the car right now. I'm taking you for something to eat," he ordered her.

"I said no," she gritted. "Are you deaf?" Dean nodded, and cricked his neck. This was the game she wanted to play huh? Good thing he was in the mood for her shit today. Dean opened the car door and tossed the flowers inside to free up his hands.

Giselle took that motion as him taking his shit

and getting the hell away from her but it wasn't. He turned around and marched directly towards at her. She stood her ground unwilling to move a bit no matter what he did or said. She wasn't sure what to expect of him but she was surprised when he grabbed for her. Going off instinct she caught his wrist and twisted it. Dean used his other hand and grabbed onto her upper arm. Giselle heard Sasha yell out but Giselle didn't break eye contact with Dean.

"So what, you're gonna hit me?" Giselle challenged, glaring at him as he had her arm in his tight grip.

"I'd never hit you Giselle," he said. "But get in the fucking car, or I'll put you in the fucking car!"

"Make me," Giselle gritted.

Sasha was in the lobby panicking as Reign ran towards her. The first thing she'd thought about was getting someone down there to help them in case Dean had gone too far and the situation escalated.

"What happened?" Reign asked Sasha, concerned. Dalen was probably at his place so Reign just shot him a quick text to get down here.

"It's Giselle!" Sasha shouted, turning to run back outside. Reign didn't know what could be happening but just the thought that something was happening made him worry about his little beauty. He followed Sasha outside with renewed vigor. To his astonishment what he saw was Giselle fighting off a large man who was trying to get her into his car. With her small body, she snaked around each move he tried to make until he grabbed her by both of her upper arms.

"HEY!" Reign yelled. "Put her the fuck down!" The man stopped what he was doing and glared at Reign. That gave Giselle enough time to wiggle out from his grip. Reign charged up to them and grabbed Giselle. He pushed her softly behind him.

"Who the fuck are you?" Reign asked him. Dean looked the man up and down. Who did this scumbag thing he was talking to? Dean wasn't about to have it.

"No, who the fuck are you?!" Dean countered.

"I'll tell you who the fuck I am. I'm the owner of this club and you're on my property rough handling one of my workers. So what the fuck is your problem?" Reign asked. Dean actually wasn't prepared for him to claim he was the owner. Still, Dean didn't back down.

"Owner of the club huh? So then that means her hours are made by you right? If you'd give my damn woman some days off I wouldn't be here having to rough her up. She's so fucking committed to you and this dumb club that she forgot all about us!" Dean exclaimed.

"Us?!" Giselle gasped. "I told you that we're not-you know what? I'm not dealing with this right now. Just know that this is pure bullshit Dean!" Giselle just sighed and walked off. Reign looked at the man. He suddenly felt some way because this was the man who got to be with the woman of his fantasies. The woman who for nearly a month Reign had to do everything in his power to act normal around. For the way the man was rough handling Giselle, Reign lost all respects for whatever kind of relationship they had.

"Keep your personal problems off my property," Reign demanded. "If you come back here and touch her again you're gonna have a problem with me, got it?" Dean backed up and looked at Reign. Even though Dean owned his own boxing arena and was very well versed in fighting, he couldn't outright punch the asshole in the face. Like he said, Dean was on his property and that would easily cause Dean more problems than he wanted to fucking handle. So the only thing Dean saw fit to do was just to walk away. He would deal with Giselle later.

Reign watched as homeboy got into his car and drove off. Angry, Reign went back into the club to find Giselle. Dalen had come downstairs to find out what happened.

"It's handled," Reign told Dalen. "Where Giselle go?" Dalen pointed to where Giselle had run off by the time Dalen had dragged on his clothes and come rushing back down to the club. Dalen had no idea what the hell had happened and Giselle didn't even stop to say anything as she rushed by him. By the look on Reign's face, he was not very happy himself.

"What the hell happened?" Dalen asked Reign. Reign only shook his head and continued walking towards the direction Giselle went towards.

"I'll tell you later. I need to check on Giselle before I flip my fucking shit," Reign grunted. Reign walked quickly to catch up to Giselle.

"Wait up little bit!" Reign called out to her. Giselle was trying to get away as fast as she could and find a place where no one was going to be in her face trying to ask what the hell happened out there. She was already in the back hall where she'd first met Reign when she heard his voice call out to her. Funny, Giselle wanted to run away from everyone but him. She slowed down and came to a stop. She took the time it took him to catch up to her to take a couple breaths and relax her heart. Once she had control of herself, she turned around just as he was right in front of her. Reign took her face in his hands.

"Are you okay?" he asked, looking at her deeply. Giselle took another deep breath.

"Yes, I'm okay. I really, really appreciate you coming out to handle that situation for me," he sighed. Reign let go of her face before he was forced to kiss her.

"You don't have to thank me. I defend the people I care about," he said. Giselle tried not to read too much into his words but hearing him say he cared about her made her swoon and blush. Then to make her further continue to lose control of her breathing, Reign took one of her arms and ran his hands over them softly, looking at the red marks from how tight Dean had grabbed her up. He did not like seeing her skin bruised up like this. He shouldn't have let that muthafucker walk away without some missing teeth.

"So that's your man huh?" Reign asked with a tint of anger in his voice. Giselle scoffed.

"I told that asshole it wasn't a commitment. I'm not ready to be tied down. Especially to someone like him. He just can't get it through his thick skull."

"I think that any man would want to be committed to you," Reign said.

"Yeah right," she sighed. "What men want from me is never what I want front them. Anyway, I have a lot of work to do I should get going. Thanks again for all the help." She went to turn away but he grabbed her hand. There was no way Reign was letting her walk away from him. He wanted to be around her some more and needed an excuse to do so.

"You've been here a long while. You're so much into your work I just saw you bouncing from place to place getting things done. I saw you get a lot of shit done today except eating something. After that ordeal outside I want you to relax a little bit and get your head clear before you get back to work. Let me get you something to eat."

"Um, well I-" Reign cut her off before she could even get her words out.

"Maybe I didn't make myself clear Giselle but I said 'let me get you something to eat', not 'can I get you something to eat.' Which means I wasn't really asking you. So, let's go." With that said, he just walked off. Giselle felt her stomach tighten and quake at his authority. Damn, she could just fuck him right then and there.

"Okay," She stammered following him like a puppy.

Reign was ready to have Khloe confront him for leaving the way he did but surprisingly she had left the office already. Reign knew he would probably have to deal with her anger later. Hell he was mad at himself because his nut sack was so sore he felt like he was on the verge of blue balls but he was happy he'd been able to protect Giselle when she needed it. She needed him more than he needed a release. With her gone, Reign could get right into focusing on his time with Giselle.

"Can I ask you something?" Reign asked her.

"What's up?" Giselle questioned.

"Does he hit you?" he asked her. She gave him a look. "And be honest with me Giselle. I won't judge you."

"No he doesn't hit me," she said. "And while I am small if he did hit me I'd fuck his ass up anyway that I could." He loved her attitude.

"Good. Cause you too sweet to be having a man hit you."

"I ain't so sweet. And besides, I take kick boxing exactly for that reason. So men don't think they can put their hands on me and I won't fight back. I could kick your ass too if I wanted," she said. When Reign snapped his head up and looked at her she winked.

"I'll keep that in mind little bit. Anyway, what do you want from the kitchen?"

"Shrimp alfredo pasta," she answered. "It's my favorite."

"No problem little bit. But you're probably going to have to eat it in your little office with the door closed, or in the dining area outside," he informed her.

"Oh." Giselle said. She was beginning to feel stupid. She thought she was going to be able to spend some time with him. Reign sensed her disappointment at something.

"I'm not trying to get rid of you," he blurted out.

"So what are you trying to do?" she asked, confused.

"I'm allergic to shellfish. Severely. The steam from it alone will make me break out in hives. Let's not talk about it coming in direct contact with my skin or if I eat it," he said. Instantly Giselle felt foolish.

"Oh shit, Reign I'm sorry. I was being selfish just then. I should have known you probably had a good reason."

"No worries little bit."

"I'll just have the chicken alfredo then," she offered.

"Sure?" Giselle just nodded. He placed the order for the food over the phone. Since she was just standing there with her arousal teetering, she decided to work on the outfits she'd halfway completed until the food was finished.

Reign watched as she put her hair in a ponytail and began working on one of the outfits she started already that was dressed on the mannequin in the corner of the room. When she bent over, Reign bit his lips as her supple breasts jiggled and shifted in her tank top. The top of her mounds were glistening in his eyes. His mouth watered as he felt blood pouring into his dick, making him rock hard.

"So you and Khloe," she said. "That's your woman?"

"Let's just say the same relationship you got with that dude is the same relationship I got with Khloe. And we've known each other for a while now. She's one of the two people in my life that is always consistent and there when I need her." Giselle nodded even though she hated that bitch.

"We need those kind of people in our lives," she said as she continued to pin and mark the outfit where it needed to be fixed or taken in. Reign continued to watch her work. When her food arrived she sat down on his couch to eat. He felt like such a pervert watching her eat, but the way her mouth closed around the fork, and the little moans of pleasure she made overwhelmed him. It was sad that she was the one making him weak when he was going to have to get his pleasure with Khloe simply because that's who he had at the moment.

# *Chapter Fourteen*

With each passing day, a slow flame burned inside of Giselle. She was so damn horny her skin always felt hot to the touch. She was going to burst if she didn't do something to satisfy her damn need. Oddly enough Dean hadn't been pressing her for any kind of sex. Giselle wasn't sure what the deal was but she didn't read too much into it. After days and days of him sending flowers and pleading for her forgiveness she'd ultimately forgiven him. She believed him when he told her that he was on a short fuse and with some things going wrong at his gym he was overworked and stressed. Giselle felt ultimately bad for not even thinking about what he may have been going through to cause him to act out the way he was. She decided that it wasn't worth causing him any more stress or problems so she just let the situation go.

Still wanting to make things up to her days after the ordeal, he waited hand and foot on her. He also took her to a spa and resort that Giselle didn't want to go to in the first place but he insisted that he didn't expect anything from her if she accepted the gift. Sasha was with Dalen all the damn time so Giselle really didn't have anything else to do but to let Dean take her wherever he wanted to.

Giselle was happy for Sasha anyways, so instead of moping around she just went to the spa. Dean had paid for her to get special attention and every special treatment possible at the resort. After all the work she was doing at the club, she didn't realize how badly she needed the pampering until she was on a massage table, having her stressmelted away. Giselle surely felt like a queen and knew she wasn't about to still be angry at a man that was catering to her like this. Only problem with that was the fact that here Dean was paying for her to have this luxury and Giselle still couldn't stop thinking about Reign. That fiery desire inside her was burning endlessly and all she wanted was just some good, pure, heavy, sex. That's it. She was seriously a woman lacking lust.

On the bright side, Dean hadn't been annoying her or guilt tripping her to fuck him like he would normally doing. At first she was relieved to not have to go through another disappointing round of sex but then she begun to find it strange. Giselle just thought that maybe it was just because he didn't want to have to argue with her again. That slow burn inside of her almost made Giselle want to initiate the sex, but she also didn't want to be disappointed. She should be happy he didn't want to have sex right? Still, it was curious as to why all of a sudden he had changed up his attitude.

With her body relaxed but her pussy wound up in tension, Giselle returned to work. With just one more day until the masquerade party, Giselle was running around the club trying to finish off outfits and decorations. This party was going to be so big the club was going to be closed that night to keep all the decorations up and ready for tomorrow night. To her, it was honestly just going to be a big fuck fest. That's what all the girls were talking about and she knew all the men attending the party was looking to get laid too. That was the exact reason why she decided she was not going to stay for the party. No way was she about to watch everyone get laid while she sat around lonely. That wasn't going to happen.

"Are you coming back to do my hair?" Sasha asked as Giselle went to leave the dressing room.

"Yes just let me get something from my little workspace," she answered. She wanted to get her book to make sure she'd done everything before taking a breather and relaxing. She would have been done with everything if these girls didn't want more than one damn outfit. But Reign asked her to make it happen, and she just couldn't say no to him.

Giselle walked quickly towards Reign's office to get to the closet she was using as her workspace. The club was quiet enough so in the hall just outside of Reign's office soft breathy moans caught Giselle's attention. She slowed down but she didn't stop walking. As she approached the office door, the sounds became more pronounced. Her mouth opened in shock when she realized her man was getting down. And yes, after long hours of working with him and daydreaming he was her man damn it! Reign didn't know of course but that didn't matter.

Giselle peeked into his office from the hallway. He'd left it slightly open as if he thought he'd closed it all the way. To him it probably wouldn't matter because the only two women that went into his office without an invitation was Khloe and Giselle. Since Giselle was running around with all this damn work he probably didn't give a second thought that she would be coming back to the office anytime soon.

And because Giselle was still horny as fuck and a creep, she peeked through the crack in the doorway to get a glimpse of what was going on inside. She tried to calm her breathing as she watched Reign's toned ass move back and forth as he fucked another woman. He was holding her in front of him, with a hand clasped around her mouth as he stroked her deeply. Tossing her down on his desk, he held her hips and pumped inside her continuously. Giselle felt her panties get soft as she heard the woman moan softly under his ministrations. When he threw his head back and shouted his release, Giselle nearly fainted. Damn he was so sexy. His body was work of muscle and art and Giselle longed to have him behind her, stroking her softly. She'd never gotten the chance to see his dick because of the position he was in, but she just knew he had to be something amazing.

With her insides quaking with arousal, Giselle dashed from the doorway. After being horny these past few days, she couldn't manage seeing what she just saw. Especially from the man she continuously fantasized about. Why couldn't she be the one he was fucking? Was it so hard to ask to get some good dick in the world? Seeing Reign fucking and orgasming sent Giselle's body into overdrive. She could hardly get her juices to stop leaking even as she walked away. She walked quickly through the main club area, sidestepping workers as they decorated the place for the party tomorrow night. She went straight to the dressing rooms and found her way into one of the stalls. When she couldn't get herself to calm down, she exited and went for her purse. Finding the fake tube of lipstick, she carried it back to the bathroom stall and shut herself in. She unscrewed the lipstick and turned on her best female toy. Her body shook and trembled with need and anticipation as she pressed the vibrator to her aching clit. She was so wound up it only took 2 minutes for her orgasm to explode through her body.

The moment she was finished, she felt terrible. She couldn't believe what she'd just done. She was driven to so much sexual madness she had to masturbate at work. That was an all-time low. How could she help it though? Every time Reign would just speak, her arousal would rise up. His lips moved smoothly, his teeth were perfect. He was built like a god. What she would give to run her hands all over his chest, and run her tongue along his lips. Giselle was pent up with all this imagination on what he would taste or feel like but she wouldn't dare to even look him at him for too long for fear he would figure out what was going on in her head. He would reject her and she would be so embarrassed. She'd never been with a man as exotic looking as him and she was downright afraid to even just tell him the truth about her feelings.

Giselle was a tiny woman with no fake parts. All of the women he messed with didn't look like her, and she knew he had a type. Just look at Khloe. What would she do? Tell Reign she wanted to be in his bed and then turn away when he began laughing at her? His light brown eyes bore through her skin and she felt the heat of his stare. He was way too intimidating. And he was way too sexy for Giselle.

Leaving the stall, she went back out into the dressing rooms and plopped down next to Sasha.

"Are you alright?" Sasha asked Giselle.

"No," Giselle snapped, embarrassed for what she had just done in the stall.

"You look like you seen a ghost."

"More like I saw Reign fucking that bitch again." Giselle shook her head and sighed. Sasha laughed loudly. Giselle didn't even understand how her friend could laugh at her in a time like this.

"I don't know why you don't just fuck him," Sasha explained. Gisele rolled her eyes. It would all seem so simple to Sasha since she had Dalen.

"It's not that easy for me you know. One, he has Khloe. And two, nothing about me is remotely attractive to him. So no, I can't just fuck him," Giselle said.

"Now shut up and let me do your hair," Giselle pouted. Sasha held her hands up in submission and left that conversation alone.

As she straightened Sasha's hair, Khloe came into the dressing room. Giselle rolled her eyes immediately knowing the woman was going to brag about having slept with Reign again.

"Whew," she said, flopping down on the chair next to Sasha and Giselle. "That dick action was bomb." Giselle couldn't help but roll her eyes again. Of course the bitch would come in here and start to brag, and shove it in Giselle's face.

"When are you gonna share some of that?" Sasha asked. Sasha only said it in a teasing manner since Khloe liked to brag, but the look on Khloe's face was serious.

"Don't talk about my man like that," she demanded. "None of y'all will ever get him. Got it?"

Sasha just scoffed and waved her off. The woman had serious issues.

"But either way, you just better watch out Sasha," Khloe snapped. She looked at Giselle.

"I'm not even worried about you," Khloe said. "Cause aren't you, a virgin or something?"

"Very funny," Giselle gave her a fake smile. "But you have it all wrong. Just because I don't go around fucking every damn day don't mean I'm a virgin. Maybe you should try it sometime," Giselle told her. Khloe started to laugh.

"Why not fuck every day when I've got a man like Reign? Maybe you don't know Giselle but the key to keeping a man is to always make sure he's satisfied. If he's not satisfied he goes to the next woman. And well Reign has a high sex drive. He loves to fuck me just as much. Who could blame him. I mean, look at me." She stood and twirled around. Giselle wasn't going to lie. Khloe's body was off the hook but it was also fake. Even so, that's probably what Reign was into if he was keeping Khloe around.

"I look like this," Khloe continued, "And you

look like a ten year old. So please, stay in your lane boo and never try and diss me."

"You think you're something because you paid for breasts and ass implants?" Giselle asked, getting mad.

"Excuse me?!" Khloe asked.

"You're a plastic bombshell Khloe but sooner or later your man is gonna want to hold onto something real. So don't think you have it all made honey. Hell, keep fucking so damn much and one of those damn implants might fucking pop on your ass and leave you looking like one of those helium balloons from the dollar store," Giselle said easily. Khloe glared at her, in disbelief Giselle had the nerves to talk to her like that.

"Bad mistake bitch. Watch what Reign is gonna do once I tell him what the fuck you just said to me!" Khloe snapped. Giselle hardly cared.

"Go ahead then! We'll see how that turns out. You walk around here tryna disrespect every damn body but then you start shaking when someone talk back to you. Ain't nobody scared of you Khloe and as quiet and polite as I may be, I will knock you on your fucking ass." Giselle gave Khloe her back and continued to do Sasha's hair. It would be easier if Sasha wasn't laughing her ass off.

"Damn Khloe, the quiet bitch you think looks like a ten year old surely put you in your place," Sasha giggled. Khloe grunted and turned the leave the room quickly. Giselle shook her head and continued to work on Sasha's hair. Khloe could go run and tell Reign what she wanted. Giselle didn't give a fuck.

"Forget that bitch. You handled her perfectly anyways. By the way, are you coming to the party tomorrow night?" Sasha asked.

"Absolutely not. I cannot stand by and watch everyone get fucked. And that goes for you too," Giselle smiled. "I know tomorrow Dalen is gonna be all over you." Sasha sighed.

"Don't worry about what's gonna happen with everyone else. You know, Reign will really notice you if you put yourself out there. Everyone knows you're way prettier than Khloe. If you really want him, I think you should put in an effort." Giselle didn't have any answers right then and there so she kept quiet. She continued to think about it as she finished Sasha's hair. When it was all done she still hadn't given her friend an answer. Honestly, Giselle didn't really have one.

"I'll talk to you later tonight," Giselle sighed. Sasha rubbed Giselle's back and decided not to push her friend any further with their conversation. Giselle left the dressing room already thinking about cozying up on her couch with a tub of ice cream. She wasn't even near the door to leave yet when she heard Khloe's voice complaining to Reign. They were walking down the hall headed for the women's dressing room.

"There she is," Khloe spat. Reign looked straight at Giselle, and she froze. She didn't move an inch under his stare.

"Shit," she cursed under her breath. Khloe and Reign approached her and Giselle stood her ground for whatever Reign would have to say to her.

"Khloe told me you said some rude things to her," Reign said. Giselle nodded.

"That's right, I did say some rude things to her. In my opinion she deserved what I said to her. You know well that Khloe is a very rude woman to begin with. I just chose not to take any of her shit. It's clear she can disrespect whoever she wants whenever she wants, but can't take it when someone decides to give her a taste of her own medicine." Reign tore his eyes away from Giselle, as hard as that was, and looked at Khloe. She had her arms crossed and was pouting so Reign new what Giselle said was true.

"Khloe, you can't complain to me after you've been rude to someone," Reign said smoothly.

"That bitch called me a plastic bombshell and said my implants were going to pop if I didn't stop fucking you! She's obviously jealous of me and I cannot work with that kind of vibe around me. None of the other girls can either." Khloe snapped. Reign's eyes went right back to Giselle. He knew she was no innocent chick but he had to admit he was surprised and turned on by her sticking it to Khloe.

"You really said that?" He asked with a smile on his face.

"Damn straight I dd," Giselle shrugged.

"Fire her," Khloe ordered. Reign looked at Khloe.

"Remember who the boss around here is," Reign ordered. "You don't tell me to fire anyone."

"My oh my, look how the mighty have fallen," Giselle said, crossing her arms. She backed slowly away from them. "Catch ya later plastic bombshell."

"Oh wait, are you coming to the party tomorrow night?" Reign asked her.

"I wasn't planning on it," she said.

"I think you should. You worked very hard to make this happen with me. You should come enjoy it." And just like that he'd changed her mind. She was sprung as fuck and he hadn't even touched her. Shame.

"Okay then sure. I'll come." She said.

"Great. If you can make these outfits for the girls, I can only imagine what kind of thing you'd wear," he complimented. It was then that Giselle realized she didn't have anything to wear. Her heart was thundering in her chest as Reign stared her down. Giselle smiled at him and turned to leave. Even if she felt confident around him, he had a way of breaking her walls down before she could even stop it. She knew if she was going to go to this party then she needed to meet his expectations.

When she got home, Dean was sitting on her porch sipping a beer. There was the man that was realistically able to be hers. Reign was nothing but a fantasy. Giselle very much appreciated that Dean was here waiting for her in the first place. After treating her to the spa and his new found attitude, there was little Giselle could really complain about.

Dean smiled at her in greeting then stood. He kissed her lips before Giselle unlocked her home and let them both inside. Dean took her purse from her shoulder and sat it on the counter. He brought her to the couch to sit down and pulled off her shoes. She was appreciative that he was here looking out for her. She began to realize she had a real life man to satisfy the cravings she'd been feeling all day instead of just relying on pure imagination when it came to Reign.

"Dean," she said softly.

"Yes?"

"I'm a little horny," she admitted. He looked at her with a wide grin.

"Oh babe, you ain't said nothing but a word!"

He kissed her neck, pushing her to lay on the couch. She came out of her underwear quickly that was still damp from watching Reign with Khloe.

"Oh wow, you weren't lying," he said as he stuck his fingers inside her. She groaned and turned her hips in time to his movements within her. She was ready to ask that he just keep it up with his fingers but then she heard him pulling down his shorts. It would surely bruise his ego if she said she didn't want his dick because he didn't last long enough.

"Get a condom," she said. When he got up from the couch to head to the bedroom, Giselle stood and took her top off and pulled her skirt completely down. She bent over the arm of the couch so the moment he walked back into the living room he would see her ass up and ready. When he walked back in and she heard the gasp she knew he got the picture. She turned and looked back at him to make sure he put the condom on. When it was secure, she turned away giving up herself to him. He grabbed onto her ass roughly and slammed into her. She yelled out from the force of the thrust not so much from the pleasure. Something had definitely changed. She had always wanted Dean to fuck her hard but with purpose. Now he was just fucking for the sake of fucking hard. Nothing about it was pleasurable. It was all pain. Of course he thought he was the shit and not that he was just hurting her.

"I know its good baby," he groaned, squeezing her bottom. Giselle just hung over the arm of the couch limply, bored out of her mind. How could she even fake it when there was nothing else for her to feel but pain and random poking at her insides? When he did his groan and shout as he came, Giselle rolled her eyes. He pulled out of her and backed away. She turned and looked at him. Here they were, yet again. Him sated and her at a loss of words for how much she wasn't enjoying his sex game. Something about that satisfied grin that was edging his lips angered her. When was this man ever going to learn? Hell, when was she ever going to learn?

"Feeling better?" He asked her.

"Lots," she said dryly. "I'm gonna shower and go to bed." She walked away from him, cursing under her breath. She was honestly getting sick and tired of the sexual disappointment.

Chapter Fifteen

It was the night of the masquerade party. The party she swore she wasn't going to. The party she had no business going to, but because Reign had asked, she easily gave in. Now Giselle's heart was racing as she walked up to the club. The line to the party was as long as ever, but being employed there she didn't have to wait. That didn't stop her from standing in front of the club and just staring. She couldn't believe she was about to walk into this damn club on this damn night and be tormented by what she couldn't have.

"Come on girl," Sasha said. "You look sexy as fuck. Time to go show it off." Giselle had decided to wear bright red shorts with a matching bustier that laced up in the front with red ribbons and perked up her breasts completely.

"Lead the way," Giselle told her. She walked next to Sasha, the heels of her black stilettoes clacking against the pavement. Giselle held her breath as she walked up to the club.

"Oh my god in heaven," Dalen gasped when he saw Giselle.

"What?" Giselle asked, feeling self-conscious.

"No, no, you look amazing girl. Damn!" He put his arm around Sasha's waist and pulled her to him.

"You looking mighty delicious yourself," he said kissing Sasha's neck.

"Save it for later," Sasha giggled.

"Fine, but remember what I told you. None of these niggas in here better put they hands on you."

"I know I know," she said. "Come on Giselle." When they entered the main room of the club, they stopped at a table set up by the door to retrieve their masquerade masks. Once they put it on, they went to the bar to get some drinks. Some of the girls were already on stage dancing in the outfits Giselle made them and wearing masks. She had to admit she was impressed with herself.

"Don't look," Sasha said. "But Reign just sat at the other end of the bar and he's staring at you hard." Giselle straightened up immediately.

"What you mean he's staring?" Giselle asked.

"Don't be stupid. I mean the man is looking at you like a piece of meat." Giselle clasped her hands together in nervousness.

"So what?" Giselle asked trying to play it off. Sasha sighed. Her friend needed a wakeup call.

"For once Giselle, stop thinking and just do. You know you want him so go and get him."

"I do, but no one said he wanted me. That's where you're missing a piece of the puzzle," Giselle said.

"I just told you he was looking at you like a piece of meat! Either you take it, or you leave it. But consider this; how many times you wanna lay in bed disappointed yet again because Dean doesn't fuck you like you wanted him to?" Giselle opened her mouth to answer, but then she closed it.

"Exactly," Sasha said. "Buck the fuck up and go take what you want or you're forever going to be disappointed." She gave Giselle one last look before she turned and walked away with her drink in hand. Giselle didn't dare turn around and look at Reign. She thought back to last night at the way she laid in bed next to a man that didn't satisfy her needs in any way. She got angry again thinking about the way he boasted about himself on how he much be doing her so good when in reality it was the exact opposite. Giselle spared his feelings by not telling him the truth about how she really felt. In sparing his feelings, she was the loser in the end. It was then she realized Sasha was right. Giselle couldn't take the disappointment anymore, and it was about time she just stopped thinking and just started doing. Giselle more than wanted Reign at this point. She needed him. And that was just the bottom line.

********

Reign was in his office bopping his head to the music coming from the club. None of the women came into the club earlier that day since they were preparing for tonight. He'd been alone all day without even Khloe bothering him. In fact ever since he stuck up for Giselle after Khloe wanted her fired, Khloe hadn't spoken to him. She'd stormed off and he hadn't heard from her since then. He knew she was okay because he spotted her in the club when he went to do rounds when the party initially started. She was entwined with some man so Reign just left her. Whenever she was ready, she would come back to him. He didn't even know why she would tell him to do such a thing as fire Giselle. Even just working here for a couple weeks, Reign couldn't imagine coming to work and not seeing her face every day. At the thought of her he wondered if she'd arrived yet. He began to wonder what she was wearing. So far Giselle seemed like a very simple girl but for the first time he'd laid eyes on her she was wearing a sexy outfit, so he knew she was capable of it.

The intercom in his office crackled again. He sat forward getting ready for one of the guards to tell him someone was either fighting or one of the girls were in trouble.

"Yo," Dalen said.

"What's up?" Reign asked.

"Your little chick just arrived. And man, you'd

better come down here and check her the fuck out." Dalen didn't need to say anything else. Reign hopped up from his chair and bolted out of his office.

When he got to the main floor, he searched the crowded club for Giselle. He stayed hidden in a corner when he spotted her and Sasha walking away from Dalen. They walked to the table to pick up a mask. Reign's mouth stayed open as he continued to watch her. She was wearing a matching bright red outfit that hugged all her curves and showed the right amount of skin. He was rock hard in his jeans as he watched her walk over to the bar with Sasha. He stepped out from his corner and sat at the far end of the bar. Again, he looked around the whole club. Through the thick crowd he saw Khloe again with that same man dancing and having a good time. When he looked back at Giselle, an alarm must have went off in his ears because he was alert to everything she did. It was then that he realized that there was nothing holding him back. The first time he attempted to show her he was attracted to her was with a kiss on the forehead she did not take well to. But with the way his dick throbbed in his jeans, he just had to try again. When Sasha left Giselle alone, Reign thought of ways he could approach her again and not offend her.

"Hey, I think you're very beautiful and I wanna taste you." Or should he try, "I'll be honest, I can see you and me in one of the private rooms getting down in about five minutes." Reign almost laughed at himself. What chance did he really have with this woman?

The bartender tapped on the bar getting Reign's attention. Reign looked at the man as he slid Reign a shot of patron.

"Not tonight," he told the bartender.

"Not from me," he shouted. Reign followed to where he pointed. His heart did that flip in his chest again as he locked eyes with Giselle. She pulled the mask away from her face and winked at him before pulling it back down. When she stood from her chair Reign thought she was going to walk over to him, but she strutted slowly towards the dancefloor.

Reign stood and watched as her waist moved in time with the music. With their eyes locked, she moved ever so slowly and dipped, staying crouched down with her legs wide open. Reign's eyes went wide at seeing the little piece of her that her red shorts barely covered.

Giselle's heart was still pumping hard in her chest. But it wasn't because she was afraid anymore. It was because she was excited she was actually doing this. After countless nights of thinking about what she would do if she ever got the chance to be with Reign, she was finally getting her chance. She could see the intrigue in his eyes and she was ready to do anything to see to it that she finally got him.

When she dipped to the ground, she saw the shocked expression on his face as he glanced between her legs. Before she could do anything else, he marched onto the dancefloor and grabbed her arms, making her stand up.

"Are you teasing me?" He asked into her ear. She smiled at him and slid down his body oh so slowly, making sure to rub herself against his growing arousal. Reign again had to hold his groan within him before he made himself look like a fool.

"Remember that kiss you gave me on the forehead?" She asked him. He nodded. "That's the kind of kiss you give to a child. Do I look like a child?" She pressed against his arousal again. Reign gritted his teeth.

"No, no you don't look like a child. I-I just didn't want to come off too strong."

"Let me show you what a real kiss is," she said. Wrapping her arms around his neck again, she kissed his lips fully, delving her tongue into his mouth. He was shocked, but he finally moaned and opened up to her, holding his arm around her waist and kissing her back softly. Giselle couldn't imagine how good he tasted and nothing she dreamt of or thought about was in comparison to the real deal. His lips were so soft for a man and yet still a little hard as well. He held her in his arms tightly, not shying away from her and not attempting to pull back. She knew he was a man in charge and was going to take what he wanted from her.

Reign pulled away from the kiss when he felt himself teetering. He was about ready to strip her naked right on the dancefloor in front of everyone. He just couldn't believe she'd been feeling the same thing he had and they both were hiding it. Now it was like he couldn't contain it anymore. He wanted her bad.

"Come with me." He took her by the hand and led her away from the party. They walked towards the back, but instead of going up to his office, he turned off and chose a vacant special room where the strippers took their guests for special activities. It was perfect. The room had a bed and everything else that Giselle wanted to use for the night.

The moment Reign closed the door to the room he didn't allow Giselle to get far. He clasped a hand around her neck and pulled her into him, ravishing her lips once more. Her knees nearly buckled underneath her, but Reign held her up and took over her mouth, kissing her deeply.

Giselle couldn't feel her body. All she could feel was Reign's deep controlling kisses. She knew that he was a man who wasn't soft and loved to fuck rough, but she was ready to take it. First, she had to drive him out of his ever loving mind. Pulling away from the kiss, she shoved him back. He licked his lips as he watched her untie the front of her bustier

Reign was motionless as he watched her undress. Her shorts came off next, revealing the garter belt that was holding her fishnet stockings up. Reign's mouth fell open as he saw that she was not wearing any underwear with the garter belt. Giselle stood there in all her glory, daring him make his move. Reign wanted to seduce her body wholly and completely knowing that they'd both been wanting this for a long time. Reign approached her and grabbed her around the waist. He walked to the bed and threw her onto it. Giselle bounced twice before she settled in the middle. For so many weeks, Giselle imagined what Reign would look like naked, and now she could barely breathe as Reign slowly began to strip. Not only did he do it slowly, increasing her anticipation; he did it like he was overly confident in his body and what he had to offer.

He was at his jeans now, slowly unbuckling his belt. Giselle leaned back on her elbows to enjoy the show. Unsnapping the button to his jeans, Reign pulled them down from his perfectly narrow hips. She licked her lips at his tight navy blue boxer briefs. Giselle was getting antsy now. He looked so damn delectable with his chest and tight stomach adorned with tattoos. His boxer briefs were barely holding down his amazing arousal and she couldn't wait to get it on.

Reign climbed onto the bed, leaving his underwear on and crawling on all fours like an Amazonian predator, to get to her. Giselle's heart was in her throat as his eyes raked over her revealed body. Trapping her beneath him, Reign attacked her lips. She moaned into his mouth and accepted his tongue. Never have she ever known a man to kiss so passionately. It sent feelings to every single crook, cranny, and crevice of her body. It was like being enveloped by a large cloud that smelled so sweet. Giselle lost herself completely in that cloud and there was nothing holding her back from delving into the pleasure and letting it take over.

Teeth nibbled, nails scratched, gasps and moans echoed through the room. Reign's tongue was everywhere, tasting each and every inch of her skin and savoring it.

"Open your eyes," Reign said lowly. Giselle pried her eyes open and looked at him. He shot her a smile, a very sexy one at that, and backed away from her, pulling her legs down with him. His arousal wasn't that well hidden behind his Hanes and seeing it strain made Giselle overly eager.

"Don't close your eyes," Reign ordered. He gazed at her long and hard for a moment before raising her knees and spreading them. Reign haven't seen a woman this intriguing in a long time. She seemed so small but she was overly seductive and he couldn't wait to get more of his mouth on her. Her lips and her skin already tasted so sweet.

"Are you watching me?" Reign asked, ready to please her even more. She nodded as he lowered himself onto his stomach, placing his head right at her center. She sat up and glared down at him. Reign felt ultimate gratification when she gasped deeply as his soft tongue went in for a taste. Oh she tasted wonderful. Peaches and cream erupted across his taste buds as he delved further into her. Giselle let her head fall back and more pleasure blossomed. This was really happening. The man of her dreams was tonguing her down something serious. This wasn't her vibrator, naw…This was the real stuff.

The things she thought his tongue could do was in no comparison to what it could actually do. On her skin, it was a warm, and a wet caress traveling across the planes of her body. She gripped the bed sheets as she writhed under the assault of his tongue. She was on the crux of release and about to shout his name, like she's done so many times with her vibrator when he bit down on her most sensitive part. She yelped and looked down at him.

"I told you not to close your eyes," Reign said. Giselle took a deep breath.

"I need you to keep going," she puffed out.

"So do as I say." She relaxed, and leaned back on her elbows, opening herself further for him. When Reign was satisfied with the way she watched him, he lowered his head to taste her again. She gasped and clenched the sheets even more to keep her eyes open. Feeling the pleasure of his long lazy laps and seeing his pink tongue play with her insides made her erupt in deep ecstasy. Even though she tried not to close her eyes, the power of the orgasm was too much. This is exactly what he wanted. Feeling the pleasure and seeing the pleasure, made her crash down twice as hard. The pleasure that coursed through her left her shivering. She moved away from his sweet lips, scrambling off the bed.

Reign loved the way he made her thrash and writhe under him. Now that was the true definition of pleasing a woman.

Giselle didn't expect to be under his mercy like that, but she had something planned for him. Some things she's always thought about doing to that sexy ass body of his.

She walked away from the bed as Reign planted his ass on the edge of the bed. Seeing her small heart shaped womanly core was making his brain fizzle and pop and he didn't know what in the world to do with this woman. He watched as she walked to the mini fridge in the room.

"What are you doing?" He asked her. She pulled out a can of whip cream from the fridge.

"Oh shit," he laughed. "You're not playing any games are you?" She stood in front of him in all her glory. Her breasts bounced naturally each time she moved.

She walked slowly to him then bent over, kissing his soft lips again. Lost in her pure seduction and her caramel kisses, Reign didn't move an inch.

"You're gonna kill me with those kisses," he breathed. He sat there watching her with heated eyes. Giselle almost felt like melting. But instead, she shook the can of whip cream.

"I love whip cream," she said, spraying some on her index finger and licking it off. Reign visibly swallowed. "But sometimes I have to eat it with something." She licked her lips and approached him. Instead of getting on her knees, she crouched in front of him, leaving legs open for him to catch a view. With the height of her heels she was at a perfect angle to handle her business. She pulled at the front of his boxer briefs and pulled it down, allowing his arousal to spring from its prison. When her eyes went wide at his size, he chuckled but didn't say anything. Sure, he was bigger than any man she'd been with, especially Dean but she knew what she was doing.

Tilting her head back, she swirled the whip cream in her mouth. Without swallowing, she came forward and wrapped her mouth around his beautifully engorged arousal. Reign threw his head back in a silent moan as the warmness of her mouth, and the softness of the whip cream coated his cock. His heart stopped for a second as she pushed his cock to the back of her throat. And just as if she was swallowing the whip cream, she began to swallow his dick and he nearly released inside her mouth. When the whip cream was gone, she sucked him up and down once before releasing him with a pop of her mouth.

"Keep sucking," Reign ordered, not ready for her to finish. She glared at him but she smiled again. Getting back into position, she put him inside her mouth and sucked him deeply. Reign fought his growing release as he watched her dip a finger into her own weeping channel as her arousal crept higher and higher. He let out a telltale sign of his release and she immediately popped him out of her mouth again. This time she stood.

"Do you like whip cream?" She asked him. Reign nodded violently. She shook the whip cream bottle again and pointed the nozzle at her perfect nipples. She sprayed a spiral of whip cream on each nipple. Holding onto his shoulders, she leaned forward dangled her lovely mounds in his face. He wasted no time capturing one of her nipples and sucking off the whip cream. She moaned softly, gripping his shoulders tightly. Even when he finished sucking off all the whip cream, he couldn't get enough of her ripe nipples. She pulled away from him, letting the nipple pop out of his mouth.

Reign snatched the whip cream can from her hand. He stood and grabbed her wrist, pulling her down onto the bed. He gently forced her to her knees, pushing her chest against the bed and raising her ass high in the air. Giselle didn't know what was happening until she felt the spray of the whip cream coat her vagina. She squealed but the moment she tried to get away, Reign fisted her ass and held her still. His tongue delved back into her channel as he devoured her once more. He wasted no time licking away at the whip cream so he could get to the best part of her.

The moment his tongue touched her clit she erupted in deep ecstasy, grabbing at the soft sheets that adorned the bed. She screamed his name and tried to get away from his tongue, but he only followed her as she moved. He licked her over and over again, sending her into another orgasm.

Her sweet juices flowed down his throat as she came repeatedly. He fucked her with his tongue each time she orgasmed to amplify her release. After her third release, he moved away from her and watched as her legs shook and trembled. When she came to, he stood up. She turned around on the bed and glared at his aching arousal, dripping with his pre-release.

"The condoms are in that drawer over there," he told her. She nodded and crawled over the bed to get to the bedside table. Pulling out one of the condoms, she came back in front of him and sat down with her legs open. Reign pushed her to lay down, and pulled her legs until her ass dangled off the edge of the bed. He raised her legs high after applying the protection to his shaft.

With one single movement their bodies were connected. Giselle shattered beneath him; achieving release from just the feel of his body within hers. Her heart was still pumping hard as she tried to catch her breath. He was so big he made her come from only filling her body completely. Reign stayed still above her, savoring how the connection felt. She was deadly tight, and Reign was worried that he was hurting her, but her muscles twitched as her release coated him. After giving her a moment to recover, he had to start moving within her before he lost his mind. He held her down to keep her in place as his movements sped up, and the power of his thrusts increased. She scored his arms with her nails, as he touched every crevice within her, steering her in the direction of another release.

Giselle was soaring. She didn't ever imagine Reign's dick would feel so good inside her. He penetrated her deep; touching a sensitive spot that made her lower belly quake with her impending orgasm. She wasn't ready to come yet, she wanted to ride him endlessly, but he felt too good. Giselle fisted the bed sheets again as he attacked her insides, clawing his way as deep as he could. She watched his large cock disappeared inside her repeatedly as he buried her into the mattress with his powerful strokes.

"Come on my dick" He growled down at her. Reign could feel her walls pulsating around him, tightening and releasing as her orgasm neared. The minute he told her to come, she shattered around him. Her legs were shaking again as her muscles contracted around him in her release.

Before Giselle could ride out the orgasmed she'd dreamt about for months, Reign let her legs down and flipped her around. He held her tiny waist in his hands. He entered her fully again from the back. Her plump bottom bounced against his stomach. That was the sight Reign wanted to see. Her pretty ass bouncing against him as he tore up her insides. He'd never made a woman scream as much as Giselle was screaming and it was music to his ears.

Giselle grabbed at the sheets in front of her and tried to pull herself from the onslaught of his power strokes. She knew Reign would feel good, but she didn't know he would feel this damn good! She was coming so much she knew the bed was soaked under her.

"Where you going?" He asked, pulling her back on his long dick. She dug her face into the mattress as she came again. "Damn girl, you're so wet!" He groaned.

"Oh Reign," She moaned softly. Reign pulled out of her slowly, watching as she tried to grip him to keep him inside.

He picked her up and placed her in the middle of the bed. Following her down, he lay in between her legs, and entered her slowly. He rested on his elbows and gazed at her as he stroked her softly. Giselle felt like they had a connection. It was just something about the way they looked at each other that felt right.

She arched her back underneath him as he slid deeper. He ran his fingers across her lips before kissing her softly. The bed slowly came to life, making all sorts of sounds under their weight. The moans erupting from her were wild and crazed. A string of curse words left her when he touched the right spot inside of her.

He caught her cursing fever as he shouted an expletive as well, drawing the word out as he began to power into her harder trying to let them achieve their releases at the same time. The headboard began to rock against the wall.

"Scream my name," he ordered. Giselle shook her head, no matter how compelled she felt to actually do it. He glared down at her and pounded even deeper. She tried not to react to how good he felt, but her release was too close not to react. She grabbed a tighter hold of him when he placed a finger on her sensitive clit. Her muscles clenched in her impending release.

"Scream it!" He shouted. Her body bucked against him and she finally erupted. Giselle screamed his name at the top of her lungs as she melted around him. Reign buried his head in her neck as her muscles clenched him and she soaked him further in her release. Giselle felt as his body shivered as his breathing deepened. He stayed on top of her for another minute, kissing her sweet lips again. It took them both some time to regain their breathing.

"You taste so good," he said, pecking her lips and then delving his tongue into her mouth. They kissed for another minute before he rolled off her. Literally, Giselle was floating in cloud nine. Her body shivered in sweet release. This was how she wanted to be left after sex. She couldn't thank Sasha enough for talking some sense into her. But now it was the aftermath. She looked at Reign as he lay still in the bed next to her.

"I wasn't expecting this tonight," he said. "But it was more than worth it to be with you."

"I feel the same," Giselle said. He raised up on his elbow and looked at her.

"I'm going to ask you not to tell anyone about this," he said. "Not because I'm ashamed," He added quickly. "Just with you, this seemed more than just a one night stand. I don't want our business floating around the girls like it meant nothing, okay?" Giselle nodded at him.

"I understand." He kissed her on the mouth.

"I can't be gone for too long. I have to get back to the club." And just like that, their special time was over. Still before he left the room, he kissed her ever so deeply as if he didn't want to leave her at all. Still, he had to go. Even when he left the room, Giselle just stayed laying in the bed. She was seriously worn out and she felt like she needed a nap. He was just that good. She hugged herself and smiled as her heart began to blossom at remembering everything he'd done to her.

## Chapter Sixteen

"How the fuck was it?" Sasha asked, as she watched Giselle gobble down cherry pie. Unlike before Giselle wasn't gobbling down the pie because she was upset. No, she was happy as fuck. Sasha knew just what that meant. Giselle had disappeared last night at the club but Sasha knew it was because she was with Reign. Sasha had spent the later part of the night in one of the rooms with Dalen.

"Lord Sasha," Giselle moaned. "That man is blessed." Sasha held her hands apart to replicate the size of Reign's dick. Giselle grinned and moved Sasha's hands further apart.

"Damn girl. You took all of that?" Sasha gasped.

"And then some! I mean, he stroked me, he licked me, he kissed me...there wasn't anything that man didn't do." Giselle couldn't help but shiver as she ate her pie.

"So what are you gonna do about Dean?" Sasha asked. "I think you should drop him like a hot piece of shit." Giselle gagged on her pie.

"Sash I'm eating!" Giselle exclaimed. Sasha shrugged and rolled her eyes.

"Anyways," Giselle continued. "I don't know what I'm gonna do with Dean. Technically it's not like I can have Reign. He's got Khloe. And I'm supposed to be trying to build a relationship with Dean."

"Yeah I getcha. But that's some shit you in. Dean can't fuck for shit," Sasha shook her head.

"Tell me about it. Besides the fact that he thinks he's got the golden dick and a slight attitude, he's a good guy. So good that he's planning to take me to some special outing this weekend."

"Well at least he spoils you rotten," Sasha smiled. "But in the end it's your happiness that matters. Not who fucks better or has a bigger dick."

"Well, isn't a big dick and good sex what happiness is?" Giselle joked. Sasha laughed and took a piece of Giselle's pie.

"You need to get your shit together," Sasha told her friend as she laughed.

********

Reign sat in his office tapping his fingers along his desk. He had work to do but he couldn't concentrate. He'd left Giselle in that room last night to finish working, but he wished he didn't. All he could think about was spending the night with her in his arms. Right now he was hard in his jeans just thinking about her moans and her perfect body. He cursed under his breath and tried to concentrate on his work. He'd gotten the checks from Tamar and he just needed to make sure they were legit before he moved on with them.

When his phone buzzed he thought it was Giselle texting him. He jumped up in anticipation looking at his phone. Disappointment flooded him when he saw that it was just Khloe. She was telling him that she was on her way. Reign didn't reply. He honestly didn't have anything to say. What he simply wanted was for Giselle to come through his office doors.

"Can I come in?!" Her sweet voice came from the other side of his door. He smiled to himself as he got up and went to the door to let her in. They looked at each other for a long moment before they said anything.

"Hi," she said softly.

"Hi." Reign let her in. She was wearing a cute skirt that flared out just reaching mid-thigh with a tank top she wore tucked in. She was so simply beautiful, Reign couldn't fathom it. Now thinking about it, Khloe's fake boobs and ass did nothing for him.

"I went to the diner earlier with Sasha. I brought you a piece of pie. I hope you like cherry." She handed him a bag. He took it and smiled.

"I do actually. Thanks," he said. "Sit." He sat back behind his desk as she took the pie from the container. Before allowing him to eat it, he watched as she went into his storage closet where he kept supplies. Since he always had whip cream in the private rooms, he kept them in full stock. She pulled a can out and shook it. Walking back over to him, she placed the pie directly in front of him. They stared directly at each other as she sprayed the whip cream neatly on top of the pie. Both of their chests were rising and falling quickly at being so near to each other. How can he think of anything but her sweet pussy when she had a can of whip cream in front of him?

"Fuck this," Reign said. He pushed the pie to the end of his desk. Pushing his chair back he grabbed onto her waist and lifted her onto the desk. She let out a cute yelp as Reign spread her legs in front of him.

"Now this is a pie I want to eat," he said. Giselle watched in awe as he dipped his head and pulled her panties to the side with his teeth. He held it off to the side and drew his tongue along to seam of her opening. He wanted to tease her and take his time but he knew Khloe would be getting here soon. He just had to feast and make it last until he was alone with her again.

He buried his head in her sweet core and sucked at her clit softly. Her body twitched against him. Fuck she tasted so good. Last night wasn't a fluke. She really tasted that good all the time. He'd given Khloe oral sex plenty of times, but she was in no comparison to Giselle on taste. The woman was a walking sugar cube. Her sweet honey dripped down his chin as he ate her alive. Her little moans were passion filled cries in the silence of the room. Reign used the tip of his tongue to swirl around her tender clit. As her moans rose in volume, his tongue flicked faster before he pulled her entire clit into his mouth and sucked her to eruption. Her hips bucked off the desk as she came on his tongue. Reign made sure to follow her, sucking her to endless pleasure. He stuck his tongue in her weeping channel to fill his belly with her toxic release. When she fell weakly against the desk, Reign kissed her soft core. She shivered, but otherwise didn't move. Reign sat up and wiped his mouth.

"Yum," he said. She giggled as he helped her sit up. She held onto him as she stood from the desk on wobbly legs. When she stepped out from in front of him, he wiped down his desk with disinfectant wipes and watched her try to get her legs to stop shaking.

"I um...I had come to talk to you about if I can get a couple days off," she said. "Not for some more pleasure, although you feast on pussy very, very well." Reign winked at her.

"You can take all the time you need after the work you put in," Reign told him. When she looked at him with a smile he realized what he said.

"I meant the work with the party," he corrected himself.

"Yes, I understood what you meant," she laughed. "So um, I'll be gone for the weekend? Is that alright?"

"Yes that's fine you deserve the time off. Let me just get you your check." Reign went into his desk for his checkbook so he could write up one for her. After he handed it to her, she set it on the desk and took a picture of the check with her cellphone to deposit it into her bank.

"And by the way I'm sorry for just jumping on you before you got the chance to say anything else to me. I just...I couldn't help myself," Reign apologized. When she licked her lips, Reign could only imagine what she was thinking.

"It's fine Reign. Do you see me complaining about it?" she smiled. "I don't think anyone should complain after getting their pussy eaten like that. Shit."

Reign laughed at the face she made. Reign realized that for the upcoming weekend he would be without her and a sinking feeling just filled him. Damn, he didn't want to be without her. Honestly, he felt really upset that he wouldn't see her for three days, but all he had to do now is be patient. Maybe in that time she was gone he could evaluate just what he felt towards this woman. Especially when it came to the fact that Khloe was still part of his life.

"I just have one request out of you before you go," Reign said.

"What's up?" Giselle asked.

"Keep in touch with me and I will be okay with your absence," he winked. Giselle smiled at him.

"Easy," she smiled. Feeling like she couldn't leave without something extra, Giselle walked back to his desk and kissed him. Just before it could get too deep she pulled back biting his lips. She could still feel his lips on hers and that just enough to hold her over. Winking, she walked out of the office quickly.

Exactly five minutes after Giselle left, Khloe

came into the office. Reign smiled and hugged her. As she talked his ear off about her night, Reign sat quietly thinking about Giselle. Already he was needing to see her, and needing to smell her sweet scent.

"Why you so distracted?" Khloe asked.

"No reason," he replied. She gave him a look.

"I think I know. You've missed me," She said. She stood and came to his desk.

"I know how you get when you don't have your daily sucking," she told him confidently. Reign immediately stood.

"No it's not that," he objected. He went to his cabinets to file paperwork. After putting the papers away instead of sitting back down, he went back to his desk where he leaned against the front and crossed his arms.

"Still, let me suck him," Khloe begged. She went to get on her knees in front of him but he pulled her up. He set her a couple of inches away from him.

"Look," he said. "I had sex with someone else last night." Her expression was shocked first, then turned into hurt.

"Why?" She asked. Reign shrugged.

"Because I wanted to," he admitted.

"Is it because I slept with someone else too?" she asked.

"No K, it's not because of that."

"So…who did you have sex with?" She asked.

"To be respectful to her, I can't tell you that," Reign said.

"You told me that you would tell me when you fucked someone else!" She snapped. Reign saw the anger seeping into her.

"Yes, and I just told you that I had sex with someone else Khloe. And you don't have the right to be mad. You told me you fucked another man and I didn't give you shit about it. We agreed on this open relationship for a reason. And believe me Khloe, if we got serious you don't gotta worry about me cheating on you. I'm not that type of man. But we're not in a serious relationship so it is what it is."

"Alright fine. If that's the way you want to do things then whatever." She crossed her arms and shook her head not at all feeling good.

"Look, I'm not working today, okay? I'm tired," she huffed. For a moment Reign felt bad for having to tell her what he did, but he'd promised her that he would. He didn't feel bad for having sex with Giselle, no he would never feel bad about that. Khloe was a big girl she'd be able to handle it.

"What the hell is wrong with you?" Sasha asked as Giselle stumbled into the dressing room. When Giselle checked that they were alone she smiled at Sasha.

"He just ate the shit out of me," she sighed.

"Oo, you nasty girl," Sasha laughed. "Reign must love him some Giselle!" Giselle hushed her when the door opened and the other girls came into the locker room. Khloe stormed in after them. She looked at all the girls.

"Who fucked him?!" Khloe shouted. The girls looked at her like she'd lost her mind. Giselle didn't make any expression even though she was laughing in her head. How could she not after the way Khloe loved to brag.

"One of you bitches fucked Reign! He told me he fucked someone. So. Who. Was. It?" She gritted. She stepped up to all the girls as if she was analyzing facial expressions. When she got to Giselle, Khloe waved her off.

"We all know it wasn't you," Khloe spat. She turned her attention to Sasha. "But I know you've been eying my man since you got here."

"You don't know what the fuck you're talking about!" Sasha exclaimed. Khloe got up in Sasha's face.

"You ain't gonna get away with this shit," Khloe threatened. "I've gotten rid of women who hit on Reign before. I will fucking destroy you." She gave Sasha a nasty look and barged out of the room. No one said anything. No one knew what to even say to begin with.

"I'll talk to Reign," Giselle whispered to Sasha. Sasha just nodded. Giselle left the dressing room and jogged back to Reign's office. She just found it so funny that Khloe was in Sasha's face but she dismissed Giselle when it was really Giselle who'd fucked Reign.

"You told her?!" Giselle snapped, entering his office. "After you told me last night to keep it a secret?"

"Told who?" Reign asked.

"Khloe!"

"Well yeah I had to tell her Giselle. Me and her are sexual partners. But how the hell you know I told her? And I only told her I slept with someone and not who that someone was."

"Well your sexual partner was just in Sasha's face talking about destroying her because Khloe thinks Sasha fucked you!"

"What?" Reign asked in disbelief.

"Yes! She's a fucking psycho and you better do something about her before she does something to Sasha or gets in Sasha's face again," Giselle warned.

"Fuck!" Reign punched his desk. "Please apologize to Sasha please. I will take care of Khloe. Don't worry your pretty head." He stood from his desk and went over to Giselle. Unable to help himself, he kissed her on the lips again further convincing her he would take care of it. Even though Giselle believed him, she knew that somewhere in the future Khloe was going to be an issue.

********

Reign immediately tried to call for Khloe but she ignored all his attempts to contact her. getting frustrated, he left his office to search the club for her. She was nowhere to be found. Reign realized that she was going to take every effort to ignore him that she could, but Reign wasn't up for the shits.

He went back to his office and continued his work so he could get things done. Later on in the afternoon when he was finished with work, he left the club and went straight to Khloe's place. Her car was in the driveway so he knew she was home and at that point she couldn't run from him anymore.

"You've got a lot of explaining to do," Reign said when Khloe opened her front door for him.

"I know," Khloe mumbled letting him in. "I figured you would come here anyway." She was wearing a fluffy robe and holding a glass of wine. Following her in the house she went to the living room to sit down. That's when he saw the rolled up tissues on her coffee table. The moment he sat down, he took her face into his hands and made her look at him.

"You were crying," he said when he saw her red

puffy eyes. She nodded. "Why?"

"I don't really know Reign, I don't. It's just a lot of emotion inside me I guess. I just don't want the mistake I made with having sex with that man make our relationship drift apart."

"Khloe, I told you me having sex with another woman isn't because of what you did. I just saw someone who attracted me and I went for it. We're in an open relationship Khloe because we're close enough to want to lean on each other but we aren't ready for the seriousness of a relationship. At the end of the day you've been with me through a lot of shit woman. I won't hold you sleeping with another man against you especially when I know we're loyal to each other but we are also free to do what we want with other people."

"I know. I realize that I'm so upset because I don't want to share you. I don't think anyone deserves you and I know for a fact that I won't be sleeping with anyone else again." Reign swallowed hard as she said what she said. A feeling of dread pooled at the bottom of his stomach.

"Reign I want commitment. I want you and only you. To be your woman, to have your babies. I want that," she said. Fear leapt into his heart. Commitment? This was the last thing he thought he wanted to hear from Khloe. At least for a while. Not when he'd just discovered the pleasure he experienced with Giselle.

"So you're saying...?" He asked her.

"I'm going to stop stripping. I'm ready to be the woman you need me to be for our future." Reign thought he would feel elation when they finally reached this far in their relationship. Only, Reign didn't feel so happy to hear it. Just when he'd finally gotten the chance to experience something new and passionate with a woman he couldn't seem to stop thinking about or finding lust like he'd never experience before, it was all going to be taken from him. With Khloe saying these words to him, he knew whatever he had or could have in the future with Giselle would come to a complete halt. He wasn't so sure he could handle that. Reign closed his eyes and sighed. What could he do? Having sex with Giselle was one of the best experiences he's ever had, but was that all it was? Was it just sex? He couldn't possibly turn away from Khloe who he'd been wanting to commit to him, who he wanted to give him children for years, all for Giselle who he had one sexual encounter with, could he?

********

To his word, Dean took Giselle on a mini vacation to relax after the tough weeks she had working. She appreciated the notion completely, and spending time in a resort in Orlando getting pampered and looked after was something any woman could ask for. They spent a day on the beach, a night on a yacht and now he was taking her to a luxury restaurant for dinner. When she'd returned from a mud bath, he'd left her a note with a beautiful dress in the middle of the bed. He wrote that he wanted her to meet him at the restaurant by 8. Giselle found it cute that he was doing this for her. But she felt like a complete bitch for having Reign on her mind the entire time they'd been here. What Giselle needed to do was break the news to Dean that she was interested in someone else. Even if that someone else had another woman who he probably would keep in his life. Giselle would probably never get the real chance to be with Reign. Here on this trip with Dean though, he was showing her that he could be the man for her that could take care of her.

No matter what went on in her head, Giselle couldn't get Reign off her mind. The two of them didn't speak even though Giselle said she would call him or text but he didn't call or text her either. Maybe he was wrapped up in his business at the club and she was wrapped up with Dean knowing well she should have been giving Dean all her attention in the first place. Even when she slept she dreamt of the onetime her and Reign had together. With getting a taste of Reign, she couldn't even fathom being with Dean sexually. It would be too much of a disappointment.

"You look beautiful," Dean complimented as he met her in the front of the restaurant. She smiled and hugged him.

"Thank you I love this dress," she smiled. They had seats on the outside deck of the restaurant. It was a beautiful night, and Giselle took none of this for granted. She was in awe of all of it and was truly enjoying herself. But this would be the right time to tell him she'd had sex with someone else. It was the right thing to do. Especially with the thoughts of Reign running rampant in her mind. She really wanted another Reign orgasm, and it was so wrong of her to be thinking about that sitting in front of Dean.

"How's your meal?" He asked her as they ate dinner quietly.

"It's so good," she smiled. He took a sip of his wine and looked at her deeply.

"What?" She asked.

"Giselle, I gotta be honest with you, okay?" Giselle swallowed hard and nodded. Dean took a deep breath before he continued.

"You're the most beautiful woman I've ever seen and been with. I am so humbled that you chose to have me in your life," he said. Giselle realized she needed to come clean right then and there.

"You are an amazing man, but I have to tell you something-" she said.

"I think I'm ready to have an amazing woman at my side," Dean cut her off. Giselle sensed trouble immediately. What was he trying to say?

"We're almost thirty Giselle. I think it's time we got really serious. We need to be real about what future we will have together." He stood from his chair and reached out for her hand. He helped her to stand.

"Is there a man out there better for you than me?" Dean asked. Reign's name crossed her mind but she shoved it back.

"I can provide for you and I can protect you. Most of all I just want you to be mine. We're not teenagers anymore and I think you need someone to be more than just a boyfriend." Everyone in the restaurant gasped when Dean got down on one knee. Giselle's eyes went wide. It was then that Giselle was slapped with reality. Back in Miami was a man who satisfied her every sexual need, but here in front of her on his knees was a man that took care of her and could possibly create a future with her unlike what Reign could do.

"Giselle Parker, will you marry me?" Dean asked.

*To Be Continued*